# LYNCHED

## ED GORMAN

BERKLEY BOOKS, NEW YORK

To Judi Rohrig

This is a work of fiction. Names, characters, places, and incidents either are the product of the author's imagination or are used fictitiously, and any resemblance to actual persons, living or dead, business establishments, events, or locales is entirely coincidental.

LYNCHED

A Berkley Book / published by arrangement with
the author

PRINTING HISTORY
Berkley edition / May 2003

Copyright © 2003 by Ed Gorman.
Cover design by Jill Boltin.
Cover illustration by Bruce Emmitt.

For information address: The Berkley Publishing Group,
a division of Penguin Group (USA) Inc.,
375 Hudson Street, New York, New York 10014.

ISBN: 0-425-19082-X

BERKLEY®
Berkley Books are published by The Berkley Publishing Group,
a division of Penguin Group (USA) Inc.,
375 Hudson Street, New York, New York 10014.
BERKLEY and the "B" design
are trademarks belonging to Penguin Group (USA) Inc.

PRINTED IN THE UNITED STATES OF AMERICA

10 9 8 7 6 5 4 3 2 1

# PART ONE

# TONIGHT

JUST BEFORE BITTER midnight, a lone rider approached the town. He had been wondering about the silence and the darkness of the place for a quarter mile now. This time of night, a prosperous town with a gambling casino and four saloons should be noisy and alive.

Now that the new century approached, there were a lot of ghost towns throughout the West, the ruins of various gold and silver booms. They were eerie places to pass through, as if all the failed dreamers and their dreams remained behind as phantoms.

The rider had the same sense about this place. Despite the three long blocks of new false fronts with fresh and sometimes garish paint, Pine City seemed deserted, haunted.

Of course, the icy November winds skittering dead leaves down Main Street didn't help. Nor did the creaking sound of loose doors banging back and forth. To the west, a wolf cried, lonesome. The rider knew how it felt. The only sound was the steady clop of his horse's hooves.

He took his time riding down the three blocks of stores and businesses. Blacksmith, pharmacy, general store, and many others, the usual run of a town of 10,000.

Racing clouds left the full moon clear for a moment. The beams shone on the marshal's badge that the tall, lean rider wore on his sheepskin. Just a few years ago, when Ben Tully had started this job, everybody said that he was way too young to have all that gray hair. They didn't say that anymore. He took his job seriously, and it had aged him.

The damnedest thing was the casino, The Golden Promise. Donnelly wouldn't close up early even if he was dying.

But the front doors were locked, the windows dark. The laughter of whores, the click and clack of dice, the foot-tapping rhythms of the player piano—that's what you expected to hear this time of night.

He rode on.

Even the livery was closed. Sometimes when a deputy was sick and Marshal Tully had to spell him, he spent a share of the graveyard shift in the livery talking to the Negro man, Archie Graves, who slept there and guarded the place at night. Archie Graves had a thousand ironic plantation tales to tell. The owners may have enslaved those bodies, but they certainly hadn't enslaved their minds and souls.

The livery was not only dark; the barn door hasp had a lock stuck in it.

Tully was just angling his horse toward the other side of the empty street, toward the small, two-story adobe building with Town Marshal painted neatly above the front door, when he saw the man sprawled in the alley next to the building.

He dropped down from his mount, jerking his Colt from his holster, and led the horse across the wide street. He tied it to a hitching post and went to see who the man was, noticing, on his way, that the front door of the marshal's office stood open. What the hell was going on here?

He'd mistaken the unconscious man for a drunk. You got plenty of those on the graveyard shift. But this wasn't a drunk; this was his young deputy, Steve Kepler. There was a deep gash across Steve's a forehead, and the way his arm was swollen, Tully thought it was broken.

He picked Steve up and carried him inside the office. The place was a maelstrom of desks and chairs overturned, of official papers and documents strewn everywhere and, most troubling, of every single carbine was missing from its usually locked rack.

He righted a chair with the toe of his Wellington boot and sat Steve down. From a ceramic pitcher, he poured a glass of water and took it to the deputy, who groaned a semiconscious response.

Quick anger shot through him when he saw the photograph of his wife Kate turned facedown on the floor, its black paper backing bearing the dusty stamp of a boot heel. He picked it up reverently. Turned it to see her face. Not a beauty, he supposed, but a bright, clever, appealing woman he loved so much that the mere thought of her could sometimes choke him up. She'd had two miscarriages, and the doctor had warned her against trying again. But she still wanted to, even at the risk of her life. God, how he loved her. She did have a somewhat mysterious past but . . .

Tully went back to the pitcher. This time he poured water onto a piece of clean cloth the office folks used for a towel.

Steve was able to drink without help. When he was finished, the simple act exhausting him, he let his head drop back. Tully moved the chair to the wall so Steve could rest his head. He muttered and moaned but said nothing that Tully could understand. The office—and the jail behind—was as strangely silent as the rest of the town. A marshal's office was typically a place for hangers-on to congregate. A lot of men wanted to be lawmen or at least thought they did. The closest they'd get was befriending the night-shift boys at the marshal's office. There were no cronies to be found tonight.

Tully used the wet cloth on Steve's forehead, dabbing away some of the scabbed blood. The cut was deep. He probably had a concussion. This sort of wound looked like the result of a rifle butt or something equally heavy.

When he was finished cleaning the wound as well as he could, he carried Steve back to the four cells in the rear.

They were empty. He put Steve on one of the bunks. Drew a coarse wool blanket over him. He'd go find Doc Daly.

He was just about to ask Steve what was going on here when he became aware of how sticky his left palm was. He looked down. Heavy, wet blood. He turned and walked back the way he'd come. Blood all over the floor—spatters, plump drops, even a few pools of it. He went back to the cell where Steve was. The bars of the cell door were gummy with drying blood.

He stood over Steve, shaking him gently. "What happened here tonight, Steve?"

"It was bad, Ben," Steve said. "Real bad."

And he started crying.

Maybe if the injured man had been just a private citizen, Tully would have let him get the crying out of his system. But he didn't have time.

He gripped Steve's face on either side and said, "Tell me, Steve. I need to know. What happened?"

"I couldn't stop them, Ben. I tried."

More tears. Whatever had taken place had hurt not only his body but his pride as well. "I did the best job I could."

"I believe you, Steve. You're a good deputy. Now tell me what happened."

"Go take a look out back."

No point in waiting on Steve any longer. Shock, shame, and confusion had troubled his mind to the degree that he couldn't or wouldn't simply say what had happened here.

Tully went through the door leading to the hallway between the cells. He walked around the blood whenever he could. The cells had been empty when he'd left for the county seat yesterday morning to testify in a rustling trial. Which made the blood all that more mysterious. Whose was it?

He pushed open the rear door and went outside, noting that the bolt had been thrown and the door was standing open. What with the turmoil in the front office, young Kepler being hurt pretty badly, and the unsecured back door—

The backyard of the town marshal's office was an open

dirt square. Sometimes, when prisoners had to be taken to the courthouse four blocks away, somebody from the livery brought over a wagon. The prisoners were taken out the back door at rifle point.

In the center of the open square was an oak tree, and it was from a heavy branch that the dead man hung.

From the angle of the man's head you could see that his neck had snapped the preferred way. Death had been quick. He wore a checkered shirt and baggy gray work trousers.

The closer Tully got, the meaner the smell got. The man had fouled himself.

Tully looked up at the face. A swollen black tongue like a nightmare rodent protruded at a leftward angle from the mouth. The eyes were bugged out but more sad than grotesque. Nothing remarkable about the face except for its scruffiness. Tully knew the face but not the name. The face vaguely reminded him of trouble. He'd run the man in a few times but couldn't remember why.

Lynching, for all that the Eastern newspapers decried it, was a part of the West. There had been a time when Tully was in favor of it in certain special circumstances, though he'd never been able to bring himself to participate in one. It was like cockfighting. He could understand it in theory, but the practice itself troubled him.

Lynching had sometimes been necessary when there was no other way to get justice. The law was either corrupt or nonexistent. This was in the early West, especially in the mining towns.

But those days were gone. There was no excuse for lynching now. There was a system of justice that was more fair than not, and a growing number of professionally run law enforcement agencies. Tully himself went to the state capital three times a year to learn modern police techniques, most of which came to the States from Scotland Yard in London.

He hadn't climbed a tree in years. He was glad nobody was around to see him do it. He didn't look like a great spec-

imen of manhood working his way to the branch the rope
had been slung over.

He pulled a bowie knife from a leather sheath on his side
and severed the rope clean. The body made a hard, dull
sound when it landed on the dirt.

He took the rope from the man's neck. The lynch mob
hadn't wasted any time on a fancy knot. They'd just wanted
to get the job done.

He carried the man inside and put him on a cot in the cell
next to Kepler. He drew the woolen blanket over the man's
face.

Then he went to question his deputy again. Maybe this
time Steve would tell him what had happened here tonight.

# THE NIGHT BEFORE

A METHODIST CHURCH group was honoring Ralph Donnelly for his contribution to the building fund. Thanks to his recent donation, the church would not only be built on time but would be able to afford fine stained glass windows and elements of marble on the altar.

Donnelly, a stout, bald man in his mid-fifties, never looked the part his enemies had long ago cast him in. Stage villains were usually meticulously dressed to the point of dandyism, affected mustaches, top hats and canes, and gave out lustful little sighs whenever the heroine appeared.

Ralph Donnelly, on the other hand, looked like everybody's sloppy uncle. Though he was easily the wealthiest man in this part of the state—he'd made his first fortune in silver and his second in vice—his business suits never seemed to fit him properly, his collars were snowy with dandruff, and his cravats frequently were stained with spatters from his most recent meal. His left eye strayed, and he was known to stutter whenever he had to make any kind of public address. He attended Mass three, sometimes four, times a week and had built a vast town hall which he named after his beloved deceased wife Ruth. There were two schools and three churches in the town, and it was largely his money that had built each and every one of them.

The Ruth Donnelly Pavilion had rung with the cheers and applause of three hundred Methodists as they rose to their feet to honor this unlikely looking town leader.

He had stuttered through five short sentences that Reverend Franklin Grace had written for him. Now, blushing from all the stuttering, he stood on the podium and waved to the people acknowledging him.

He was just about to sit down again when he saw young Deputy Kepler come into the pavilion, looking flushed and anxious. While Donnelly and Ben Tully were enemies of long standing, Donnelly had tried to develop a good relationship with Kepler. He sent birthday gifts to Kepler's children and anniversary gifts to him and his wife. Mrs. Kepler always wrote short but grateful thank-you notes in a sweet, feminine hand.

Kepler came halfway up the aisle between the chairs gathered in front of the podium. People whispered about his rudeness, barging in this way, and about how frantic he seemed.

He said, "Excuse me, Mr. Donnelly. I'm sure sorry to interrupt you, sir."

"I'm sure it's for a very good reason, son."

With these words, everybody relaxed a little. If this interruption was all right with Donnelly, it was all right with them.

"Is there something you need, son?"

"Yessir. There is." You could see how flustered he was. It made him look even younger and more vulnerable.

"Tell us what you came here to say, son."

A lot of the ladies smiled at the warm, paternal way Ralph Donnelly was treating the youngster. Say what you wanted about Donnelly running all the liquor and whores and gambling in town, and say what you would about how the newspaper was always championing Ben Tully's attempts to send Donnelly to prison, Donnelly was at heart a decent man. How many other so-called vice lords would build the churches and schools he had? And where was the money coming from for the new hospital? Ralph Donnelly, of course.

Deputy Kepler angled himself so that he could address both Donnelly and most of the congregation. His freckled face with its snub nose and large teeth was almost ugly with agitation.

"A woman's been found dead. Raped and murdered."

The dime novelists liked to make the West out as a coarse land of incessant violence. But the West was no different from the East. The people here wanted—demanded—safe streets and the right atmosphere for raising families. Rape and murder got the same fearful, angry reaction here it would have in New Hampshire.

"I'm going to need as many men as I can get to sweep the woods behind the house. See what we can find."

"You can count on me, son," Donnelly said. "How many men here will join us?"

The cottage was on the east edge of town. The picket fence and the swing in the front yard contrasted with the events that had taken place inside. A plump woman was crying silently into a handkerchief, occasionally blowing her nose into it. She'd stopped by to see her friend and had found the body.

The men assembled outside the gate of the picket fence. They carried rifles, shotguns, lanterns, torches.

Deputy Kepler sure wished Ben Tully was here. At least he was up on methods of detection, including how to sweep an area for pieces of evidence. Kepler read some of Tully's crime method magazines from time to time but not regularly or seriously. He could more often be found sneaking off with a copy of *The Police Gazette*.

"We're looking for anything that the killer might have left behind," Kepler said, sounding callow and nervous in the vast, chill night. His breath plumed silver in the darkness. "And we're also looking for the killer. Some of you probably remember last year when Sheriff Culligan over to Benton Junction found that killer hiding out in a barn.

Sometimes, that happens. They get scared and they hide. Let's do everything we can to find him."

There was a fine edge of anger in the voices of the men. A thing like this could happen to any man's wife. There was always a monster lurking somewhere. Your luck depended on whether or not your wife happened to be in his path when the craziness set upon him.

"We'll fan out and meet back here in . . . three hours," Deputy Kepler said, wishing he had a deeper voice, like Ben Tully's.

The first thing he did was vomit.

That was frequently the first thing he did.

The second thing he did was take a piss.

That was frequently the second thing he did.

Then he set to wondering where he was exactly.

This was bad enough, but there were nights—nights when he'd been drinking straight grain alcohol—when he woke up wondering *who* he was.

He was standing in a shallow, leaf covered gully next to railroad tracks that gleamed golden in the misty, pale moonlight.

Railroad tracks made sense because it had become the fate of one Francis Xavier Conners to spend his life riding the rails. Railroad tracks and the culture they spawned had become his home. Sleeping in boxcars. Getting chased and sometimes cruelly beaten by railroad dicks. Sharing food in hobo jungles. Going on the mooch door-to-door in passing towns.

And that was when he felt the blood on his right hand. And *felt* was the right word. It chafed there, burned. Because it wasn't his. Because feeling it made his mind start to flood with shards of memories. Terrible, terrifying memories. Stopping by a house to mooch food and finding—

From behind him, a voice said, "You better go wash yourself up down to the creek, Francis. Same way I did. Nobody better see us with blood on our hands."

Bert Lawson walked around in front of the six-and-a-half-foot giant, Francis Conners. Lawson's dark and shabby clothes marked him as a hobo, too. "Somebody's gonna find that woman pretty soon, and people's gonna come lookin'. They find a pair of 'bos with blood on their hands . . ."

Conners strained to remember. That was the thing about blackouts. You could've done anything, and your mind was incapable—or unwilling—to tell you.

A cottage. A pretty lady. Bert getting mad when she wouldn't give him any cash, even after she given them huge slices of cherry pie and stout glasses of milk, Bert getting mad and—

Conners heard them before Lawson did. A hunting dog and several men. But Lawson saw the lanterns before Conners did.

Neither man had to say anything. There was nothing to say. A posse had formed. A posse that would be delighted to come upon a couple of 'bos. Especially one with blood streaked all over his hands.

They'd both seen it happen before—'bos ripped apart by the hands of angry mobs.

"Best way to handle this," Lawson said, his voice trembling, "you head east, I head west. That'll confuse the dogs."

"I told you, you shouldn't ought to've done it, Lawson. Asked her for money."

"No time for that now, Francis. Run, now. Run as fast as you can."

Lawson wasted no time taking his own advice. Soon he was a sprinting shadow against the Western night.

Conners tried to run, but he didn't get far. He was so woozy from his hangover—hell, he was still drunk was what he was, so drunk that no amount of cold night air and pure stark terror could sober him up—his foot found a gopher hole, sending him crashing to the ground. He slammed his head so hard, he felt consciousness slipping away. . . .

He forced himself to stay awake, aware. Then the pain started radiating up his leg from his ankle. Not twisted. Broken. Conners sat up against great, blinding pain and felt his ankle. Swelling already; a raw jut of cracked bone.

He could hear a slow freight coming down the tracks. He was good at jumping freights. Knew how to do it without getting himself killed. This freight was gonna take him out of here. This freight was gonna save his life.

He stood up, or tried to, and knew then that this wobbling, rattling run of boxcars wasn't going to save him, after all. Because the pain was such that even standing up nearly made him black out. If he tried to run on his ankle, he'd only make it a few feet before he collapsed. He'd busted it good, he had.

Frantic search for somewhere to hide. No culvert. No tree. No shanty or shack left behind from the days when the railroad tracks had been laid.

Men and dogs closing in. On the hill behind him now. The dogs barking at first scent of him.

Of all the damned luck—his ankle.

*Told Lawson just to leave—told him and told him and told him.*

Just as other 'bos over the years had told him about Lawson. *"That man is trouble, Francis. Pure plain trouble. You hear me, Francis? Pure plain trouble."*

"Look, down there!" somebody shouted.

Conners could see them silhouetted against the moon—six or seven of them carrying lanterns, torches, shotguns—looking like huge and ancient warriors against that ageless circle of light, dogs in the lead, dogs ready to tear him apart if their owners didn't demand that privilege first.

*Never should've taken up with that damned Lawson. Never should have.*

And then they set upon him in all their sweaty, whiskied fury, and there could be no doubt that his life was over.

# TONIGHT

STEVE KEPLER SAT up, took the shot glass of whiskey Tully offered him. Life shone in his blue eyes for the first time since Tully had hauled him in from the alley.

"How you feeling?"

"Got one hell of a headache, Ben, I'll tell you that."

Tully was about to start asking more questions when a voice behind him said, "I brought the doc, Steve, in case you needed him."

Ralph Donnelly and Doc Daly stood on the other side of the bars. "Saw you in the alley there, Steve, and I went right away and got the doc."

Daly was a stooped little man with a tobacco-stained white beard and an impatient manner. "He looks all right to me; his arm's not broken."

"Maybe you should examine him first before you say that," Donnelly said.

Daly sighed. "I got some real sick people at the hospital, Donnelly. A lot sicker than this one here."

"You know who beat you up, Steve?" Tully said.

Tully was used to the fealty young Kepler always paid Donnelly. He knew Donnelly was trying to befriend Kepler, play him off against his boss Tully. So the sharpness of Kepler's words surprised him. "Maybe you better talk to Donnelly here, Ben. He can tell you all about it."

"What the hell's going on here?" Tully said, looking in turn at all three men.

Donnelly and Daly glanced nervously at each other. "You mean nobody's told you?"

"I just got in from the county seat and found a man hanging from a tree out back and my deputy laying unconscious. That's all I know." Then: "And why does Steve here want me to ask you what's going on, Donnelly? You have anything to do with that lynching?"

Donnelly, always in quiet command, said, "You check on young Kepler here, Doc. The marshal 'n' me'll go up front and have drink."

Tully wasn't sure why, but he went along with Donnelly's plan. He didn't like the way the man's self-importance, low-key as it was, seemed to fill the entire jail. Nor how that self-importance seemed to intimidate even Tully tonight.

They stepped into the office. Or what was left of it. They righted two chairs and sat amid the mess. Tully fished a bottle of bourbon from his bottom desk drawer. He found two unbroken glasses. The bourbon had been a gift from a grateful rancher. It had remained unopened for two years.

"You actually like this whiskey?" Donnelly said.

"We're not here to talk about whiskey."

"Let me send you over a bottle of good mash, Tully. Keep it here in your office for special occasions."

"I'm going to ask you again, Donnelly. You have anything to do with that lynching tonight?"

"You better get a hold of that smart lawyer of yours."

"You would've done the same thing I did."

"I'm a lawman, Donnelly. I don't go in for lynchings."

Donnelly's fleshy face folded into an expression of real sadness. "Kepler didn't even tell you that much, did he?"

"I don't know what you're talking about."

Later, Tully would remember the way Donnelly said it.

Flat out, with no attempt at being dramatic. Just plain and simple. Stating a fact.

"Your wife was raped and murdered last night, Tully. We wired you at the court house this morning, but you were already gone. About four hours after it happened, the posse turned up the man who did it. He had blood all over his hands, and he had a bunch of odds and ends from your house in his pockets."

A lawman frequently gave bad news. Over the years, he got more practiced at it. It never became routine, but the telling got more skilled. As did the way he handled the shocked and grieving recipients of the news.

But Tully had never prepared himself for receiving bad news of his own. His first impulse was to argue. Say they must have gotten the wrong person; no way Kate was dead. His second impulse was to accuse Donnelly of enjoying this. An old enemy finally got to watch Tully shatter. His third impulse was to go berserk in the way an animal might, rage and revenge and madness overtaking him as he finished demolishing what was left of the office.

He made a noise of misery he'd never heard before. He startled himself with it—part bleat, part cry, part sob.

Kate was dead? That was impossible. Just damned impossible.

He said, "Where is she?"

"Over to the funeral home."

"Was she dead when you found her?"

Donnelly nodded.

"The man admit it?"

"The man?"

"The man you lynched."

"He started crying and said he was so drunk he couldn't remember if he'd done it or not. But he had blood all over him, and he had the things from your house."

Tully leaned forward. The chair squeaked. "You're guilty of murder."

"I'm willing to face it."

Tully studied the other man's face. Donnelly seemed truly moved by what had happened to Kate.

Donnelly said, "I lost my own wife a couple years back, Tully. There isn't anything that can prepare you for the grief you're going to go through. Sometimes, you'll think you're losing your mind. Nobody knows this, but I tied one on one night and tried to kill myself. But the gun slipped and I missed. I guess when I thought of all that . . . I wanted him dead. A man who'd do something like that to a good woman like your Kate . . . I'm willing to face whatever you decide to do, Tully."

Tully watched him carefully. "We hate each other, Donnelly. Why would you care what I have to go through?"

Donnelly smiled. But the smile only made his sadness seem more real. "Maybe someday you'll believe that there's a little decency in me, Tully. I hope so, anyway. I sure do hope so."

He killed the rest of his drink, stood, and walked out.

As for Tully, he made it nearly all the way home before the tears came and the big hands became angry, useless fists.

# ONE

TULLY'S IDENTICAL TWIN stood in for Tully at the wake. Stood in for Tully next morning at the burial. Stood in for Tully at the ham dinner in the church basement after the casket had been put into the ground.

That was how it felt to Tully, anyway. As if he were standing off to the side watching someone else endure all the social niceties of death. A sad nod for the clucking, commiserative ladies; a stern handshake for the men who, like him, were embarrassed by tears and ritual. The only difficult moments for the Tully stand-in was when somebody said, "You'll find somebody else, Ben." No way to describe how angry that made him. As if loyal, loving mates were all over the place, easy for the pickings. And what did it say about him? That the dearest person he'd ever known—he tried hard not to remember her face the times after she'd miscarried, her grief overwhelming to him even now—that the dearest person he'd ever known meant so little to him that he'd already be thinking of her replacement?

A couple of times, he had to hold himself back from swinging on the person who said it.

Night became day became night became day.

• • •

His senior day deputy, Mack Byrnes, ran the office. He was a handsome man—women were always flirting with him—with wavy blond hair and hard blue eyes. Solid, competent, trustworthy. He was the best, driest lawman in town. Maybe even better—smarter, sharper—than Ben Tully himself. He was younger and, unlike Tully, a high school graduate.

Mack came out to the cottage on a rainy Saturday afternoon, bringing his wife Susan along.

Susan—a once-pretty woman who was fading now in her thirties, from hard work—took Tully in her arms in a maternal way and held him for a long moment. He enjoyed the comfort of her body, her goodness, more than he wanted to admit. He saw himself as a lone, stoic figure, but he wasn't. He had always needed a woman, and sex was the least of it. He trusted women more than he did men and considered them smarter and more reliable in most respects.

After their embrace ended, Susan inventoried the cabin and found it wanting. Brushing pale blonde hair back from her freckled frontier face, she said, "I'm taking the wagon on into town to the general store. I'll pick a few things up for you there, too."

Mack and Susan's eldest daughter, Delia, came in. Fifteen, with the good looks, almost aristocratic, her mother had once possessed. Not even the loose, faded blue shirt and the sloppy dungarees could hide her ripening body.

She came up and shyly touched Tully on the arm. "I'm sorry about your wife, Mr. Tully."

He kissed her on the forehead. "Thanks, Delia. I appreciate that."

"I'm gonna come clean your house in a few days. With my mom."

"You don't have to do that."

Susan spoke up. "No, we don't have to, you're right. But we *want* to." She laughed. "You're not going to arrest me if I get you some groceries are you?"

He tried a smile. "I've got an empty cell at the jail. Plenty of room for a nice-looking woman."

Melancholy darkened her eyes. "Been a while since I've been nice-looking, Ben, though it's sweet of you to say."

Then she was in his arms again, holding him tight, her blue gingham dress smelling clean and fresh. He'd sometimes wished that Kate had been as open and knowable as Susan here. There were things about Kate's past that she'd never talked about. She tried to give the impression that her past wasn't really all that interesting before she'd ended up here in Pine City, but he'd sensed otherwise. That may have been why Kate and Susan had drifted apart as friends. They'd been inseparable at first, but Kate's reluctance to ever share much about herself pushed people away.

Just then a voice from the doorway said, "Are we going now, Mom?"

Louise, at twelve the second oldest Byrnes girl, and a pretty one, too, wore a dress identical to the one Susan wore. Susan sewed all their clothes.

"I'll be right along, honey. I just wanted to say good-bye to Marshal Tully."

Then, as if realizing how funny the scene must look to Louise, she pulled gently away from Ben.

Louise stepped into the cottage, went over to where her father was at the table, sorting through papers he'd brought along, making several thin stacks.

"Tell Mom we should go."

Byrnes looked up at her, took her to him. "What's the one thing I told you that you had to work on, honey?"

"Patience."

"That's right. Patience.

"Your mother and Ben here are talking. Now why don't you say good-bye to the marshal and go and wait patiently in the wagon? We waited for you while you got your horse fixed that day. And that took quite a while."

Louise sighed. "All right, Dad." Then, "I'm sorry I busted in here like that, Marshal."

"I'm glad to see you, honey."

Louise was just turning to go when she saw the walnut-framed photograph of Kate when she was in her late teens.

She took it in slender hands. "Gosh, I think I've seen this somewhere before. It's so beautiful of her, Marshal."

Byrnes looked uncomfortable, obviously sensing that talking about the photograph might upset Tully. "Why don't you put the photograph down and run out to the wagon and wait for your mom now?"

"It's all right," Tully said. "She was a beautiful woman, Louise. Thanks for saying that."

"Well, I'll be waiting outside. You want to come with me, Delia? Good-bye, Marshal."

Delia said, "See you in a few days, Mr. Tully."

Tully nodded.

"Sorry, Ben," Susan said when the girl was gone.

"Nothing to be sorry for."

"Kids aren't always—"

"It's fine, Susan. Really."

She glanced around the cottage again. "Louise and I'll do a little straightening up and sweeping when we get back from the store."

"Susan, you don't have to."

"There you go again, Ben. I know I don't have to. But I want to. All right?"

She came close enough to give him a peck on the cheek and then went over and did the same to her husband. "See you boys in a couple of hours."

Byrnes had brought the arrest records and the monthly budget to catch Tully up-to-date. But that wasn't the real reason he was there, and they both knew it.

Tully had cuts of wood burning in the fireplace. His Irish setter, Sundown—so named because of his brilliant red coat—lay in front of the flames, luxuriating. Tully was drinking beer and reading an adventure novel. His eyes no longer looked teary. But he looked gaunt, spooked by a lack of good sleep and filled with a Poe-like melancholy.

"Mayor asked me to bring you this letter," Byrnes said when he'd finished off the official business.

"Figured I'd be hearing from him."

"He says he wants what's best for you," Byrnes said. A hesitation. "And the town."

He got up and walked across the floor to Tully's chair. Handed him the envelope.

"You read this yet, Mack?"

"Draft of it. I asked him to change a few things."

Byrnes went back and sat down in the armchair.

Tully put the letter in his lap and stared at it. "I won't shit you, Mack. I'm too confused right now—too damned raw— to make sensible decisions about things. That's why I turned things over to you."

Byrnes just listened.

"I don't have to read this letter, do I? I mean, I know what's inside, don't I?"

"Pretty much, Ben."

"He doesn't want me to bring any charges against Sieversen for instigating that lynching or for Donnelly not stopping him."

Byrnes said carefully, "How he said it to me was, 'The way most people in this town figure it, Ralph Donnelly did him a favor.' "

"I expected he'd see it that way."

"He says Sieversen and Donnelly hanged the man who killed your wife. And that you should be grateful to them and forget all about the lynching. He doesn't want you to co-operate with the investigator the state's attorney's office is sending out."

Rain made pocking sounds on the roof. The fire hissed and popped. Sundown yawned a couple of times. Tully stared at the envelope.

"What would you do, Mack?"

"About Sieversen and Donnelly?"

Tully nodded silently.

Byrnes sighed. "I won't bullshit you, Ben."

"I don't want you to."

"I think they did the right thing."

"For the town?"

"For the town. And for you. He's stopped by to see me a

couple times, Ben. I don't like him any better than you do. I got a kid brother spends most of his paychecks at the Golden Promise and lets his kids go hungry. That may not be Donnelly's fault directly, but he sure as hell doesn't discourage it."

"But your answer is he did the right thing?"

"I don't see how else to look at it, Ben. He spared you and the town the trouble of a trial."

"We're supposed to be lawmen, Mack."

"I know that. And ordinarily, I'd agree with you. But in this case . . ." He hesitated again. "I'm just glad you didn't have to go through a whole trial, Ben. And I have to agree with the mayor. I hope you don't try and bring any charges against Donnelly or Sieversen for this."

The silence again.

"I'm going to need another week, Mack."

"Fine. Take it."

"You're doing a good job, and I appreciate it."

"You'd do the same for me."

Tully surprised both himself and Mack. He turned in his chair and sailed the letter back to Mack. Unopened. And then he smiled. The first smile since hearing of Kate's death. "You tell the mayor that cooler heads prevailed. Namely yours. I guess maybe Donnelly and Sieversen did me a favor after all," Then: "By the way, any more on that stagecoach robbery?"

Byrnes shook his head. "Afraid not. And Sam Carter's there raising hell every morning, wanting to know where the robber is."

Carter was a local merchant who sold jewelry, among other items. He'd been coming back from the state capital with more than $5,000 in gems and cash. Five, ten years ago, stagecoach holdups were common. But with the railroads now, they were rare.

"Somebody had to know Carter's schedule, the way I figure it," Tully said.

Byrnes said, "That's the trouble. He stands over at the saloon after work and gets a couple beers in him and tells everybody everything. Half the town knew he was going to buy jewelry at that auction."

"Well, just tell him we're doing the best we can."

Byrnes grinned. "That's what I tell him every morning, Marshal. But he's sick of hearing it, and I'm sick of saying it."

There was the rainy morning Sundown came in all wet and hairy, looking dopey and dear. And Tully laughed. Really laughed. There was the night when he awoke at two A.M. to find himself with an erection. The first in the three weeks since Kate's death, the first he'd been aware of, anyway. There was the afternoon walk along the bluffs with the river below when the clear, clean aromas made him tear up, not with sorrow but with simple joyous appreciation. Food began to taste good again. His evening pipe satisfied once more. Some of the weight he'd lost in seven weeks returned to flesh out his face and shoulders and ribs. There was still that distant melancholy in the blue eyes, but both his deputies and the townsfolk began to recognize him once more. Life drags you back, gives you no choice. You either become part of the passing parade of your time, or you die, sometimes spiritually, sometimes physically. Though a part of him wanted to do just that—he had begun to think sentimental thoughts about graveyards and about spending eternity with blue jays and cardinals and dignified little wrens on the swell of ground around his headstone, lying next to beloved Kate forever. But clamorous life would have none of it. He had a place in the parade, after all, and he'd damned well better get in with getting in step with the music.

The ninth week following Kate's death (he had begun to mark time from that date) was a busy one. A misguided bank robbery; a warehouse fire that claimed the life of an old drunk who'd been sleeping inside; the drowning of a six-year-old boy; an unhappy poker player following the winner home and wounding him in the shoulder; pigs getting loose from a wagon and raising hell on a fine, sunny morning all over the shopping district, the merchants not happy about having to clean pig shit off their boardwalks.

And Tully was caught up in it, happy to be released from the worst of his gloom. It would imprison him again, to be sure, usually late at night, but the daylight hours were becoming a trustworthy friend.

He was working on the monthly budget—anything his office required beyond the sum the town council budgeted had to be requisitioned at an open, public meeting filled with taxpayers who thought that the town marshal's office already got too much money anyway—when Mack Byrnes brought in the morning mail.

Since his ascension to senior day deputy, Byrnes had been ordering himself dark suits from the Montgomery Ward catalog (or Monkey Ward as most folks called it). He looked pretty spiffy for a 140-pound, five-foot-seven Irisher with a fist-busted nose and an unruly mess of blond hair.

"Ted Forbes missed work again last night, Ben."

"I saw that on the roster."

"You want me to talk to him?"

"You're too tough on him, Mack."

"All the work he misses, maybe I should be tougher."

This was the only side of Mack Byrnes Tully didn't like. He could get sanctimonious. He figured since he'd given up the bottle, everybody should take care of their problems, too. But sometimes problems had a way of resisting even the best efforts.

"He'd be better off if that wife of his would leave him once and for all."

"Maybe you're right, Mack. But it's not our place to tell him that."

"So we let him miss work?"

"He doesn't miss that much work. Just when she runs around on him. And he really does get sick. I've checked up on him. He runs a fever, and he's got it coming out of both end, and he's pale as all hell. But when he's here, which is most of the time, he's a good man. We should keep that in mind."

Byrnes smiled. "Am I wearing my Roman collar again?"
That's how Tully always said it "Take off your Roman collar, Mack."

Tully nodded. "Sometimes it gets a little tight on you, Mack. You have to remember that not everybody's as strong as you are."

"You're as strong as I am, Ben."

Tully shrugged. "I'm not so sure of that. I'm really not." He pointed his pencil at the credit and debit sheet he was working on. "I need to get back to work here."

Byrnes turned and walked to the door.

"You think you can talk to Ted and keep in mind that he's good man and a damned good deputy?"

"I won't even take my Roman collar along."

"Good. Ride out there and see how's he doing."

He spent another half hour on the bookkeeping sheet. He needed to update the carbines. Some of the outlaws he had to chase from time to time had better weapons than his own men. But he would have to do some juggling to please the taxpayers, show them how he could cut corners over the next six months to pay for the weapons he needed now.

He didn't give the mail a thought until he was finished with his bookkeeping sheet. Then he rolled himself a cigarette, put his boots up on the desk, and proceeded to work his way through a considerable stack of mail, most of which went right into the metal wastebasket on the right side of his desk.

The only material he spent any time with was the monthly magazine, *Modern Police*, which dealt with scientific detection. He wasn't sure he was smart enough to understand most of it, but the arts he did understand were exciting, especially the material on fingerprints, which law enforcement people were just now starting to use. Fingerprint evidence had been struck down by all courts, but the magazine insisted that someday even the courts would have to recognize the method for the valuable tool it was.

Soon, he was down to four unopened business-size letters. He ran through them quickly, deciding by the printed names in the upper left corner that he wouldn't bother opening any of them.

The last letter, hidden behind all the others, was smaller than business-size and written in a smart, careful hand. It reminded him vaguely of Kate's writing style, and for a moment the old grief came rushing back.

He opened it.

Marshal Tully,

I am the sister of the man who was hanged in your town. His name was Francis Xavier Conners.

He was an innocent man, and I have proof. I will be in on the 407 from Denver this Wednesday at approximately 9:50 A.M.

I will come directly to your office.

Sincerely,
Nan Conners

# TWO

THE FIRST TIME Ralph Donnelly ever caught his younger brother Frank at it, they were young boys. Ten or so.

There'd been a storm coming up, and Frank was down by the creek somewhere, and Ralph had been sent to bring him home.

He'd wanted to scare the kid—you know the way kids like to scare each other—and so he crept up quietly as possible.

Frank, who was a shy, quiet, good-looking boy, was sitting hunched over doing something to the underside of his right arm.

Ralph's first instinct was that Frank was making some kind of Indian sign on his skin. Prairie boys loved playing Indian.

But then he heard Frank's sob of pain. Whatever he was doing to himself, it hurt like hell.

And then he smelled it. He'd never smelled it before—not human flesh—but he'd sure God smelled plenty of *animal* meat burning before.

And then he saw the stogie. And it all came clear to him.

And he stood that day on the prairie, the darkening sky black and frightening, the temperature dropping steadily, the stink of the devil upon everything, and he wondered why his kid brother would take a stogie and burn himself this way.

He didn't find out that day, not the *why* of it, and he didn't find out in the coming years, either. Two, three times over the coming decades, Donnelly put Frank in asylums, especially after Frank killed that girl outside Phoenix. Took $1,000 cash to pay off that lawman. And then he'd had to promise the lawman that he'd keep Frank locked away the rest of his life. But Frank escaped. And came running back to his brother-protector, the only true friend he'd had in his whole miserable life. And he promised Ralph that there would never be another "incident" again. Not ever. By then, Donnelly had built his first mansion. "There's plenty of room for me, Ralph. And I won't bother anybody, I promise. I promise."

But Ralph's beloved had warned him. "Not his fault he's crazy, Ralph. But he's gonna drag us down, drag our whole family down, take away everything we worked so hard to build, Ralph."

Frank was good about one thing, anyway.

Whatever kind of things he did, he didn't do in Pine City. He went on "trips." They never asked him where he went or what he did. But when he came back, he always seemed rested, sated.

But then something had happened the night Tully's wife was murdered. . . .

The kid had stumbled home reeling drunk and covered with blood, and he'd climbed straight up the grand stair and gone to his room without a word, and then the sobbing started.

Finally, Ralph knocked on his brother's door. Louder and louder. Angrier and angrier.

And Frank staggered to the door and said, "I saw that lynching last night, Ralph. They lynched the wrong man, Ralph. The wrong man."

And then he fell, sobbing, childlike, utterly helpless, into the paternal arms of his big brother.

"The state investigator wasn't very happy, Marshal." The mayor smiled. "And we appreciate you helping to *make* him not very happy."

"I don't feel good about it."

"Justice is justice, Marshal. Sometimes, it isn't pleasant to behold."

"As long as it was the right man."

"Oh, it was the right man. There's no doubt about that." He'd been in Mayor Cryer's office for ten minutes. The mayor had wanted to congratulate him for frustrating the state investigator's attempt to charge somebody with the lynching. No name had been turned over. The town suffered from a general amnesia, it seemed. Nobody remembered anything about the lynching, whose idea it was, who had slipped the knot around the big man's neck, who had slapped the horse's rump. Couldn't remember a damned thing.

"Somebody has some doubt," Tully said. He pitched the letter onto the mayor's desk. A narrow man with a pocked, angular face and a bad tobacco hack—you never saw the mayor without his cigarette—he represented the middle-class merchants of this town, the ones who stood against Donnelly and his casino and his saloon. They didn't like vice. They didn't seem to have any trouble with lynching, though. Some of the city's finest gentlemen had hanged the man. Tully knew why he went along with all this. Because they'd killed the man who'd killed Kate.

The mayor read the letter and said, "You know what you should do?"

"What?"

"Meet this Nan Conners at the train. And then put her on the next one out. Send her right back to where she came from. You know how these people are. They just can't bring themselves to admit that anybody they loved so much could possibly do something so bad."

"I agree. That's the way these things usually are."

Cryer, who excited easily, said, "You saying this one's different?"

"I'm just saying I want to hear her out."

Cryer fell back in his tall executive chair. "Hear her out and then set her ass on a Pullman seat and send her back to wherever the hell she came from. That's what you need to do, Tully."

Tully stood up. He lifted the letter from the desk top, folded it and put it back in its envelope, and then slid the envelope in his suit jacket.

"I still don't like lynching."

"He killed your wife, Tully."

His eyes fixed on the mayor's. "I hope he did. Because if he didn't, two innocent people died."

Ralph Donnelly always went to confession on Wednesday morning, when Father Flaherty sat in his confessional two hours following Mass to accommodate the old people. Being a mining town, there weren't that many old people—nobody wanted old miners or old whores or old gamblers—but there was a sufficient number for the priest to hear them at a special time. Saturday afternoons, when everybody else came, was frantic and always ran long. Why make the old ones endure that?

One thing you had to say about Donnelly, he would have made Rome smile. Hard as he was, crooked as he was, violent as he sometimes had to be, he never missed Sunday Mass unless he was sick, and he never missed weekly confession, either. He'd spent his first ten years growing up in the old country near Dublin, and a man never changed after that experience.

There were certain benchmarks in Donnelly's years of confessing. The first time he'd ever touched a girl's naked breast, for instance. The first time he'd ever broken a man's arm. The first time he'd ever stolen a substantial amount of money. The first time he'd ever shot but not killed a man. The first time he'd ever shot *and* killed a man. And so on.

He remembered each of these times, how his mouth had been dry, refusing to form words; how he'd sheathed himself in cold sweat; how his hands had trembled. An eternity in hell was nothing compared to the anxiety he felt in the darkness of the little confessional, the scent of flowers and incense in there with him. Eternal hell was nothing compared to the rage of the priests he confessed to. There were moments when he thought they'd come bursting out of the confessional and grab him right out of the booth and start stomping on him. He listened in shock and shame as they gave him penances that would take forever to say. And demanded, when the sin was injuring or killing someone, that he turn himself over to the authorities, something he never managed to do. He was a businessman, and he did what was necessary. There was no malice in what he did and, anyway, the people he trucked with (and killed when the time called for it) generally needed killing. At least as he saw it.

This morning, in the darkness of the confessional, Donnelly was about to make another memorable confession. But he wasn't sweating, shaking, or experiencing an inability to speak. The old priest would not thunder at him. The old man was not just getting up there in age (eighty), he also suffered from partial blindness and palsy. He just wanted to get through confessions as quickly as possible. And he knew how much Donnelly gave to St. Patrick's. Indeed, there would *be* no St. Patrick's if Donnelly hadn't built it and continued to support it.

An old one on the other side of the priest was just finishing up her confession. She spoke very loudly. She made Donnelly sad. Sweetness always moved him, and she was undeniably sweet, her sins so minor—falling asleep in Mass once, scolding her cat too harshly, thinking an unkind thought about her dead husband, saying "dammit" when she spilled her tea—that she was a virtual angel. The priest must have been moved by her, too. Her penance was one Hail Mary. Donnelly had never heard of a penance so meager.

The far door of the confessional opened. The old woman made her careful way out. The confessional window slid open on Donnelly's side. He could smell the whiskey on the priest's breath. The white-haired, fleshy old man was never drunk, but then again, he was never far from it, either.

"Bless me, Father, for I have sinned," Donnelly began. He spoke briskly, going through all the familiar sins of a man of his age and inclinations, and then he said, "I'm not sure if this is a sin or not, Father."

"Tell me, Ralph, and I will help you decide."

"I know of someone who did something terrible, and yet I haven't gone to the authorities."

"I'm not sure if that's a sin, Ralph, though you should talk to this person and ask him to go to the authorities himself."

"There's more, Father."

"Oh?"

"I caused another man to be killed."

The priest cleared his throat. Donnelly hated the gross sounds of age and infirmity. He knew they could be upon him soon enough.

"I'm afraid I don't understand."

"I had the power to stop him from being killed, but I didn't."

"This was the hanging a while back?"

The old man was sharp.

"Yes."

The priest sighed. He sounded upset. He'd never been upset with Donnelly before.

"They hanged an innocent man?"

"Yes, Father."

"Oh, my Lord in heaven."

"I don't feel good about it."

"You *shouldn't* feel good about it."

"Father, please keep your voice down."

"I want to see you in the rectory."

"When?"

"When? Right now."

"I have a meeting I need to go to."

"I don't give a good damn about your meeting. You meet me in the rectory in five minutes."

*The rectory I built*, Donnelly thought.

He felt like a small boy who had just done something very stupid. He'd thought there was a way of simply hurrying all this past the priest. And having the old man absolve him of all blame for the lynching, something he could've stopped if he'd taken the responsibility.

Now the old man wanted to see him. He was going to get reamed the way he had over his first wonderful feel of bare tit. Or the first exhilarating time he'd ever stomped somebody.

The most powerful man in this part of the state was about to get his ass kicked by a boozy old mick from Galway Bay.

She used to stand on the edge of the depot platform and watch the trains pull out and wish oh so fervently that she could be on one of them. She'd wear a picture hat and a blue dress of organdy, and her hair would be put up the way they wore it in all those magazines she liked to look through. And she wouldn't have the deep scar on her right cheek, and she wouldn't always feel embarrassed and ashamed of herself for not being as good as other people. Her mom was always saying, "Just because we're poor don't mean we ain't just as good as them stuck-up people, honey." But she knew better, and so did Mom. In fact, when Mom was cleaning houses for rich people, she sometimes took Nan along, and it was stomach-turning awful to see how Mom bowed and scraped to rich people, always fluttery and nervous and apologetic around them. It made Nan Conners sad. She knew *she* wasn't as good as those stuck-up rich people. But she knew that her *mom* was. And much prettier than any of those fancy women, too.

Nan remembered her mother's funeral. A year ago today. "She died of wearing out," the doctor had said. "She just plumb wore out, Nan. I'm sorry." And so she had. Six kids to raise and no husband, the mister's body still being somewhere down in a collapsed mine shaft these eighteen years, God rest his soul.

She was glad that neither Mom nor Dad had lived to see

Francis Xavier hanged. She smiled. What a sissy name for a strapping six-six man who could pick up an anvil with one hand. But with absolutely no tolerance for alcohol. Three drinks, and he'd become a madman, and he consequently got himself into a lot of trouble. He hadn't been mean or violent, but he had liked his fun, and his type of fun was sometimes misunderstood. The thing was, people were just plain threatened by his size. And so he was in and out of jails. He might have been different—less inclined to "fun"—if he hadn't traveled the rails with Bert Lawson. Bert lived through Francis Xavier. All the things he was afraid to do himself, he had Francis Xavier do for him. And Bert had a very lively mind when it came to cooking up things to do.

But neither Bert not Francis Xavier were killers. Of that Nan was sure. And she had a letter from Bert Lawson saying that, telling the real story of that night. Nan had tracked him down right after the lynching. Lawson was in a county jail for stealing bread from a bakery. The local lawman had let her talk to Lawson. And he'd given her a letter explaining how they'd come to be in the dead woman's house that night.

This was the letter she was carrying to a man named Marshal Tully in Pine City.

"Care for some chocolate?"

There were advantages and disadvantages to being as pretty as Nan was. Even with her scar, many men found her well worth pursuing. She wasn't sure why—her clothes were poor, she wasn't especially well spoken, and she was mortally shy—but accepted it for both the blessing and curse it was.

"No, thank you."

The man across the aisle in a bowler was probably ten years older than Nan's twenty-one. Every twenty minutes or so during the 200-mile ride, he'd offered some sort of confection or other. And he told her about himself. Well, what he mostly told her about were the things he sold. He was a drummer, he said, and proud to be one when he was the exclusive representative in this part of the country for such products as Dr. Scott's Electric Flesh Brush ("Beautiful Skin

Guaranteed"), Dr. Scott's Electric Hairbrush ("Your Scalp
Will Say Thank You"), and Dr. Scott's Electric Toothbrushes
("Permanently Charged Electro-magnetic Charge Right In
The Handle"), *electric* being the most popular word in the
entire vocabulary these days. If a product wasn't electric, it
was clearly a lesser item.

"Girl like you, hard to believe you haven't been caught."

"Caught?"

"Sure. By a handsome young man."

"Oh."

"Or," he said coyly, plump face and too-small bowler at
rakish angles, "a little older man who may not be so good
looking but's got his feet on the ground and some money in
the bank."

She was playful, which surprised her. "Now who could
that possibly be?"

He blushed, which she found sort of nauseatingly endear-
ing. She didn't hate him as much as she had a moment ago.

"Well," he stammered. "Who I had in mind was—"

She felt sorry for both of them in this awkward moment.
"I guess I'll get some sleep now."

"Yes," he said, his face still flushed. "That sounds like a
good idea."

No picture hat. No organdy dress. No hair put up so fancy
and all.

All her dreams of exotic and romantic train trips.

A stammering sad drummer.

And a letter that she hoped would incline the marshal to
look into her brother's death. Poor Francis Xavier. So big
and so misunderstood. It really was God's mercy that her
parents hadn't lived to know that their son had been
lynched.

# THREE

TULLY HAD NEVER been a social person. Dancing embarrassed him, long nights of conversation bored him. But in the last few weeks of his time without Kate, he found himself sitting in the Pine City Café for two, three hours at a time. The light and the human noise held off the darkness of his time alone. The women who worked there all joked to themselves about how dutiful the marshal had become, complimenting them on their hair waves and their dresses and especially on their prompt service.

He felt especially close to a gal named Irene. Her buggy had tipped over in a rainstorm one night, and he'd had to swim into the river to rescue her. It hadn't been all that dramatic or heroic—chances of either of them dying that close to shore were damned unlikely—but Irene treated it as if he'd been Custer standing off the Sioux all by himself. Her husband, even more grateful, practically broke into tears anytime and anywhere he laid eyes on Tully.

*Clink, clatter, clamor:* good, warm, satisfying café sounds.

This was Wednesday, Swiss steak night, and that just happened to be the cafés speciality, so the place was packed.

Tully had his usual place at the end of the counter, reading the weekly papers from surrounding counties, rolling cigarettes from time to time, and pushing his cup forward for coffee refills.

Once, when he glanced up from his newspaper, he felt someone staring at him. A lone man in a good brown suit watched him and then looked quickly away. Nothing familiar about the man. Thirty, maybe, wavy brown hair, full mustache, nice enough looking. Nothing special here. People always stared at the town marshal. People were always taking his measure, trying to read something in his face.

He decided to treat himself to a slice of apple pie. The piecrust here was something special. He forked it down with childlike pleasure. He was finishing up his last cup of coffee—he was one of the lucky ones who could drink coffee right up till bedtime and sleep well anyway—when he saw the stranger in the brown suit stand up, leave a tip, and start toward the front of the café. Their eyes met, held. Tully had the uncomfortable feeling that the stranger knew something important about Tully, something he didn't mean to share. Tully didn't like either the feeling or the man.

He walked home. He was not a horseman. You had to ride the damned things, but he did so as seldom as possible. Easterners always supposed that all Westerners loved equines. Not so. Tully found a good many of them to be damned disagreeable and unreliable. He had gone on horseback to the county seat only because he'd wanted to get back home for Kate's birthday, and the train schedule wouldn't allow it.

He enjoyed walking in all but bitterest winter. Tonight was cold, but that only seemed to enhance the beauty and majesty of the brilliant stars and the half-moon. His cheeks chafed, his breath plumed, his nose tingled. Pleasant memories of such nights with Kate, especially when they'd first started courting. They'd walked in rain, sleet, snow, one night even in punishing hail. New love made you oblivious to such things. All you cared about was being with her. And when you weren't with her, you lived in a kind of nether-world. No color was quite as vivid; no sound quite as pleas-

ing; no joke quite as funny unless she was there to imbue
everything with her personality.

Of course, that kind of love can't last. A different, deeper
kind of love evolves.

Once again, he began to think of their final three months
together. The trouble in her eyes that she never speak to; getting up in the middle of the night, sitting at the window, and
staring out; and suddenly crying without reason, the clamor
of her grief filling him and shaking him.

What had been going on with her those last months?

He tried to push those thoughts aside. He wanted, needed
sleep. Coffee might not keep him awake, but thoughts of
Kate sure did.

The houses he passed looked enviably snug. Husbands
and wives, children and dogs and cats, families. All inside
and cozy and warm for the evening. He had a terrible moment of self-pity and then forced it away. Yes, he'd lost
Kate, but people lost people all the time. He hadn't been singled out by any dark forces. A drunken madman had killed
his wife in a frenzy.

He was just thinking of the letter he'd received this morning—the woman oh so convinced that her brother was innocent—when he put his hands inside his jacket pockets for
warmth.

At first, he wasn't sure what it was. He tried to guess simply by feeling it. A fragile chain of some kind and a smooth
piece of metal attached to it.

He was just a block from his cottage when he took it out
and held it up to the moonlight for inspection.

A locket.

Now how the hell had that gotten into his jacket pocket?

Only one logical answer. The café. He'd hung his coat on
a peg near the front of the place. There'd been a couple of
dozen other coats there, too.

Somebody had intended the locket for one of the other
coats and had slipped it into his by mistake.

He'd drop it off at the café when he went there for breakfast in the morning. He was just about to open the locket

with his thumbnail when the dog belonging to his nearest neighbor came rushing up to him, eager to be petted. She was a big, sweet-faced collie. He gave her a full three minutes of rough and playful affection.

He got inside, lit a lamp, lit a fire. He had yet to take his coat off. Then he remembered the locket. He took it out, carried it over to the lantern, parted the halves, and looked inside.

He recognized her immediately. Lovely Kate, his wife. Very young, maybe eighteen, before he'd met her.

He recognized the man in the facing photograph, too. He looked much younger, too. The man in the café tonight who'd been staring at him.

Now the question became: Who the hell had slipped the locket in his coat and for what reason?

He meant to find out just who had slipped that locket in his coat.

He woke up several times that night and lay there frustrated. Obviously, the locket photographs implied that Kate and this man had been special to each other. Who was he? Where had he come from? And exactly what *was* his relationship with Kate?

And what about Kate? She'd always told him she'd grown up in St. Louis and come out here with her aunt, who lived in Canyon Junction, eighty miles to the west. From time to time, she went to visit the aunt. Tully had never thought anything of it. But now . . . there must have been a dozen such visits in the eight years of their marriage. Had they *really* been to see her aunt? And now that he thought about it, it was funny that he'd never seen the aunt, nor seen any letter she'd written Kate, nor heard Kate talk about her unless a visit was imminent. She'd always portrayed Aunt Helen as so sickly and infirm that Tully hadn't even wired the woman to tell her that Kate had been killed. He was afraid that it might destroy what was left of her health.

But today, he would wire her. And today, he would start looking for the man in the café. He suspected that the man himself had dropped the locket in Tully's sheepskin. Playing some kind of game. Teasing him for some reason Tully couldn't understand but was determined to find out.

He slept in sweaty fits the rest of the night. When it was time to go to work, he felt as if he hadn't had any sleep at all.

*She* would *have to be pretty*, Tully thought. *Damn her.*

Given the night he'd had, everything irritated him this morning. The winter day was too beautiful, the prisoners in the drunk cell too loud, the streets had too much manure in them, he had an inexplicable ache in his lower back, and the top of his left hand was itchier than hell and for no apparent reason. He needed to relax, but he'd already had three cups of coffee, and relaxing was now impossible.

She was no beauty, but she was fetching, a word he'd heard a ham actor use once in a play, and a word he'd treasured since. You met beautiful women and pretty women and cute women, but you rarely met a fetching woman. Tully couldn't even have told you what *fetching* meant exactly, but he knew it when he saw it, and she was fetching, all right.

His reaction was complex. He felt guilty because he was grieving for Kate and shouldn't have noticed if the woman was fetching or not. And he felt irritated because being so fetching, she was going to be much more difficult to dismiss than if she'd been just a nice, normal woman. And he felt slightly cowed because he knew he was outgunned already. He was a small-town marshal. What sort of defenses could he put up against fetching?

Then she turned toward him—he'd been able to see only the right side of her face—and he saw the scar, and he felt a whole lot better. Yes, she had beautiful coppery hair, and yes, she had a lost-kitten sweetness in her face, and yes, she had a comely young shape inside her dark blue traveling dress and jaunty little hat. But she also had a long, ugly scar on the left side of her face that changed everything. Still

fetching—very much fetching—but fetching with complica-
tions. Fetching, but not *perfectly* fetching.

And that made him feel one whole hell of a lot better
about himself and about her. He didn't even feel irritable
anymore, which had taken some doing.

He walked up to her. She'd been the only young woman
to disembark. She carried a carpetbag in one hand and an
umbrella in the other. Just the way she moved marked her as
a creature of big cities. There was just the faintest hint of
contempt in her eyes as they assessed what she could see of
the town from here and of the man making his way toward
her.

"Nan Conners?"

"Yes. Marshal Tully?" She put out her hand. City women
were always shaking your hand.

They shook.

"I'd be happy to carry that for you."

"No, thanks, it's not that heavy. I'd appreciate it if we
could go right to your office so I can show you this letter."

"You wouldn't like to get a hotel room first or have something to eat or—"

"Plenty of time for that later. I'm not here on vacation,
Marshal. I'm here because you hanged an innocent man."

"I wasn't even here."

"I didn't mean you personally. But your town hanged
him. And he *was* innocent."

She was even more formidable than he'd expected. She
couldn't have weighed one hundred pounds, but it was like
doing battle with a 300 pounder swinging a club. She had
that kind of grit and determination. She also had a cause, and
she was a true believer in that cause, and true believers were
the most tireless foes of all.

"Well, then," he said, making his voice as deep as possible to show that since he was wearing the tin and since he
was of the male species and since this was his town, he was
in charge here. "Well, then, why don't we go over to my office."

•  •  •

Frank came down to breakfast in his ruby-red silk lounging robe. The time was ten A.M. His brother Ralph had been at the dining room table, where all their meals were taken, for the past hour and a half. He'd been going through the mail, something he always did before going to the office.

"Little early for you, isn't it?" Ralph said, making the sarcasm as blunt as possible.

As he said this, he winked at the maid, who'd come out to take their breakfast order. She smiled.

"Will you both have the usual?"

"Yes. And I saw that smile. You'd better be careful, sweetheart, or I'll tell my little brother about all the things you and I do up in my bedroom."

Rosarita giggled. She was a short, squat woman in her sixties.

Ralph knew how to kid people. And they liked it. Coming from him, anyway. Frank was too clumsy to try things like that. He could be sarcastic but never deft.

Rosarita brought coffee, and breakfast began. There was talk of the casino and talk of one of the new croupiers; there was talk of some of the ruffians who'd been raising hell lately and talk of a dance hall girl who was apparently stealing from some of their most important gamblers. Talk and talk and talk. As usual. Frank always pretended to listen intently (though he'd retain none of it, and had no interest in how the casino ran, just as long as he got to stroll around in his new clothes looking important). And Frank always pretended that what he was saying was important, too.

Ralph tried to pay a little more attention as they talked this morning, Rosarita coming with basted eggs, sliced fried potatoes, a generous slice of beef, Rosarita returning with some kind of pastry she'd made just for Frank, Ralph not having his brother's sweet tooth. Ralph was watching his brother carefully for any sign of anxiety or nervousness.

The night of Kate Tully's murder, Frank had come home bloody and blackout drunk . . . and had never showed the slightest hint since that anything was wrong.

Perhaps it had been a coincidence. Drunks were always

falling down and breaking bones and cutting themselves. And they usually had no recollection the next morning of how they'd done it. Part of the drunk's life, nothing more.

And God knew how many times Frank had smashed himself up and had to have bones mended and cuts tended and wounds bandaged.

But still . . .

Ralph said, "You've been acting funny lately."

Frank lifted a forkful of pastry to his mouth and said, "I have?"

"Like something's on your mind."

Frank glanced toward the hall. "I don't want to talk about it. Maybe later."

"Something happened, didn't it?"

Frank finally put the pastry in his mouth, chewed carefully, and swallowed. "No." And then he looked at his brother.

"You're a bad liar."

Frank sat back in his chair. "What *should* be on my mind?"

"You've just been acting funny is all."

"Funny how?"

"Oh, like you don't pay attention."

Frank laughed. He was terrible at emulating his brother's casual, dismissive humor. "I never pay attention, brother. You should know that by now." A sip of coffee. "Anything else?"

"You've been calling out in your sleep."

Frank showed interest in their conversation suddenly. "I have?"

Donnelly didn't know what nerve he'd struck, but he'd sure struck something. "When I walk by your door in the morning, I hear you."

"What do I say?" Edge in his voice now. Trying to make a joke of it. "Anything incriminating?"

"You sound desperate. Scared. Sort of frantic."

Frank usually looked comfortable to the point of arrogance in his sleeping robe. Too rough to be effete but with an air of idle, rich smugness. Not now. He was leaning forward. "Anything you could understand?"

Ralph said calmly, carefully, "Anything we should be talking about, brother?"

"Don't be ridiculous. I have a few nightmares, and you're accusing me of something."

"Strange choice of words. *Accusing.* I'm just trying to find out what the fuck is wrong with you."

"Well, that's what you were doing, wasn't it, accusing me of something?"

"I just asked if anything was bothering you was all. You were the one who used the word *accusing.* Not me."

Frank spent a moment gathering himself. "Well, this is a stupid conversation, isn't it?"

"Is it? I just asked you if everything was all right, and you start coming apart."

"I'm not coming apart. I just don't like accusations."

But how the hell would Frank have gotten hooked up with Kate Tully? She wouldn't have anything to do with a man like him. Even if she hadn't been married to Tully.

Frank threw down his cloth napkin. "This is one hell of a way to start a day, isn't it?"

"I didn't mean to upset you."

"I'm not upset, and quit saying I am."

But Ralph stabbed his brother one more time. "Well, you act upset. You sure do act upset."

Frank was on his feet. "I'm going back to my room. I try and eat a nice little breakfast, and look what the hell happens."

Ralph said, serious now, cold and blunt, "Something's bothering you, Frank. You know it, and I know it. Maybe it's time you think about telling me what it is. Maybe it's something I can help you with."

"If something *was* wrong, brother, you'd be the last one to know about it. I'm sick of you trying to run my life. I can take care of myself."

"I hope that's true," Ralph said, "for both our sakes."

# FOUR

"AND BERT LAWSON is who exactly?"

"My brother met him when he took to the rails."

"Your brother was a—"

"Hobo, I guess you'd say."

"Any particular reason why?"

"I guess I don't understand."

"A lot of hobos are running from things. Marriages, debts, the law—things like that."

"Not Francis Xavier. He just wanted to see the world."

"That's what he was called? Francis Xavier?"

"Yes. People called him that kind of as a joke."

"He didn't resent it?"

"No. He liked it. When he was a boy, he always talked about being a priest. He always said he'd be called Father Francis Xavier."

"What happened to his becoming a priest?"

"Girls. He started falling in love all the time. Or what *he* called falling in love, anyway. He'd get all tangled up with a girl, and he'd get so smitten with her that he'd lose weight and couldn't sleep and couldn't work or anything. And then he'd meet somebody else, and the whole thing would start all over again. I always felt sorry for the girls. He would've been a good catch, my brother."

"Why?"

"Why? Just his size alone. Six foot six. A big Irisher with a strong back and a lot of gumption when he needed it. He'd have been a good provider. And he was a kind man, too. Gentle."

"I telegraphed some of the lawmen in the area. Seems Francis Xavier wasn't always gentle."

"If you mean, did he like to have fun, yes, he certainly did. But he wasn't mean, and he wasn't violent toward other people unless they were violent toward him first."

"He spent a lot of weekends in jail for drunk and disorderly."

"Drunk and disorderly, yes. But that doesn't make him a violent man, does it?"

"No, I guess not."

"And it certainly doesn't make him a killer. He would never have hurt that woman, let alone killed her."

"In the letter you showed me from this Bert Lawson, he admits they were both there."

"It's like Lawson says, they were on the tracks when they saw this sort of isolated place. They were hungry. They decided to ask for food, the way hobos do, before they lit out of town. But when they got there, they found this woman on the floor. She was already dead."

"The woman was my wife."

"My God. I never made the connection. Tully and . . . Tully. My God. I'm sorry. I didn't mean any disrespect."

"I know that. Don't worry about it."

"I really am sorry, Marshal."

"Let's go back to this letter from Lawson."

"He wouldn't have any reason to lie. Francis Xavier's already dead."

"He has *every* reason to lie."

"I don't follow."

"He can also be charged with the murder."

"But they hanged Francis Xavier for it."

"They can hang more than one person for a murder, you know."

"I guess I never thought about that. I just assumed you'd taken Lawson's word that they didn't kill . . . your wife."

"The county attorney wouldn't be very happy if I told him we were closing the case solely on Lawson's word. The feeling here is that your brother and Lawson killed my wife. The county attorney will want Lawson brought back here."

"I sure don't like Lawson. He kind of had Francis Xavier hypnotized. Francis Xavier always thought Bert was so much smarter than he was. But I believe Bert when he says they didn't kill her. I wish you believed him, too, Marshal."

"I don't know what I believe. I like to think I have an open mind on the subject."

"I know Francis Xavier. I know he didn't kill anybody. He couldn't. It wasn't in his nature."

"Not even when he was drinking?"

"Not even then."

"Not even if Bert Lawson told him to?"

"He'd do just about anything Bert told him. But not that."

It was terrible what he was doing, he thought. Using his wife's death to keep this fetching young woman talking. He'd already dismissed the letter. He hadn't been kidding about the county attorney. William Dowling would have a couple good laughs over it and pitch it into his wastebasket. Tully wanted to bring Lawson back here and talk to him and then make up his mind. There was still the mysterious locket and the man in the café, too. He had no idea what that was all about.

"Your mind is starting to wander."

"Beg pardon, miss?"

"Your mind. It's wandering."

"Oh."

"Women generally pay better attention than men."

"And you base that belief on . . ."

"Experience."

"I see."

"Men think they know the answer even before you start

talking. So they think they don't have to listen carefully. So their mind wanders."

"Not all men."

"Not all men."

"Thanks for agreeing with that."

"But most."

"You don't like men, Miss Conners?"

"The men I like I really like. But there aren't many of them."

And then she started crying. It was so abrupt, it startled him. She just sat there, fetchingly fetching, and tilted her head with its jaunty little hat down at an angle, and cried soft, silver tears and said, "I just keep having nightmares about it. How it must've been when they were putting the rope on his neck, And how he kept screaming he was innocent. And they wouldn't believe him. Even. Though. He. Really. Was. Innocent, I mean."

From her sleeve she took a lace handkerchief, dabbed eyes, nose, corners of mouth. "I promised myself I wasn't going to do that."

"It's all right."

"Men hate to see women cry."

"You seem to know a lot about men." His voice was harsh, irritated. Then he smiled. "Or think you do, anyway."

"I guess I had that coming. I . . . had a bad experience with a man . . . a fiancé—and I guess I've started thinking that all men are like he was."

"You couldn't be more wrong, Miss Conners." He smiled again. "Men are a wonderful lot when you come right down to it."

"You have a nice smile."

"I'll bet you do, too. You'll have to let me see it sometime so I can make sure."

So she let him see it.

"Even nicer than I expected," he said.

"I'm sorry about your wife."

"Thank you."

"But Francis Xavier didn't kill her. I know he didn't."

"Maybe Bert Lawson killed her."

"Much as I dislike him, Marshal, Bert didn't kill her, either. I know he didn't."

"I appreciate your coming here with this letter, Miss Conners."

"You do?"

"Sure, I do. Now I know where to find Bert Lawson."

He walked her to the front door of the station. When he came back to his office, it seemed awfully empty, as if a party had just ended. He knew why. Her presence had downright excited him. He felt guilty about being excited, of course, but he couldn't help liking it, either.

"Everything's fine with the merchants," Mack Byrnes said. One of his jobs as senior day deputy was to make the rounds of the merchants and make sure they were all happy with the marshal and his men. There had been a time in town, before Tully, when doors had been left unlocked and burglary was an ongoing problem. Tully changed all that.

"Nice-looking girl," Byrnes added.

Tully looked up from his desk. Paperwork. This time it was forms the state required filling out. And only the marshal himself could fill them out. Just once he wanted to see a dime novelist put in a scene where a lawman spent a morning or an afternoon filling out forms.

"Yes, she was."

"What'd you think of her?" Byrnes said.

Tully tossed his pen down, leaned back, and put a hand to his yawn. "She makes you want to believe her."

"Her looks don't hurt. But I wonder where the hell she picked up that scar."

"Yeah, I doubt it was accidental. Somebody took a knife to her, looks like. Anyway, she has this letter." He told him about the Bert Lawson letter. "She seemed to think that because her brother was hanged, nobody would bother going after Lawson. She thought he was just doing her a good turn with the letter and all. She seemed surprised when I told her he was probably just trying to make things look good for himself."

"What'd the letter say?"

Tully shrugged. "This Lawson and Conners—Francis Xavier, as she calls her brother—they were just a pair of hungry 'bos who went up to my cottage to beg some food. They wouldn't have stopped there but it was near the railroad tracks. So they went in. Kate was dead when they got there."

"Or that's what this Lawson says, anyway."

"That's what he says."

"You going to put her on a train the way the mayor said?"

"I figured I would," Tully said. After a moment, he said, "But I don't think so."

"Why?"

Another shrug. "Because the lynching always made me uneasy. Maybe they got the right man, but maybe they didn't."

"I could give you their reasoning, Marshal. I probably shouldn't say it, but . . . it makes sense to me. You find a man with blood all over his hands and things stolen from your house."

"Yeah, it does make sense. And it's probably true he did it. Or they did it, more likely. But . . . well, I just don't want to run her out of town cold that way."

Byrnes grinned. "Welcome back to the living. I'll tell Susan."

"The living?" Tully said. But he knew damned well what Byrnes was talking about. He felt his cheeks color.

"Susan said, 'First sign of interest in a woman, you'll know he's getting better.' And this is the first sign." Tully liked Susan Byrnes very much. And her brood of five tow-headed kids.

"Well, don't go marrying me off just yet, Mack. For one thing, believe it or not, I'm still in love with my wife. All right?"

His words had come out fiercer than he'd planned. But Byrnes had embarrassed him and made him feel guilty. He'd been taken with the young woman, no doubt. But he sure didn't want to admit it. Not with his wife scarcely buried. It wasn't any subject to be playful about.

"I didn't mean any offense, Ben," Byrnes said. He always called him Ben at the most serious moments. "I was just happy for you."

"No offense intended, none taken," Tully said. "Now I'd better get back to this paperwork."

Mack nodded and left.

# FIVE

THE WAY MARY Kay Washburn saw it, her boarding-house yielded her two things: money and power.

The money, of course, came from the boarders: eight of them, all men, and mostly railroad men, either too young to be married or else widowed. Mary Kay Washburn (who was, if you asked her, holding her own pretty darn well in both the face and the bosom departments) preferred to have males only, because that ensured she was the center of attention. Men were born to flatter a pair of breasts; they did it as a kind of reflex. Even women they didn't find especially attractive at first came to appeal to them, at least a little bit, as time wore on. And in this case, they gave her money to boot. Her late husband—whom she hadn't liked all that much (did he *have* to pass gas when they were making love?)—hadn't left her with much insurance. And he'd left her a mortgage on the house. So what choice did she have but to take in boarders? She was making the bank payments promptly and even setting a little by, thank you very much.

Power was a more subtle reward than money. She was not as young and pretty as she once was, perhaps, but she still

maintained a strong sexual hold on all her boarders. Or so
she believed. They all fancied her, they did. One sight of her
splendid bosom, and they had no will left. And that wasn't
her only kind of power, either. She made a point of knowing
a few things about each and every one of them. Secret
things. Useful things.

It wasn't difficult, at least not most of the time, to know
things about her people. Here she was, home all day long
while the men were out working.

Not difficult at all to slip up to a room. Not difficult at all
to use her passkey. Not difficult at all to go through bureaus,
closets, desks, carpetbags.

The biggest scandal at the moment belonged to Mr. Jaffer.
He was colored, but he was passing. She couldn't *tell* anybody he was colored because a person of the male boarder
persuasion might just say, "No way, Mary Kay, I ain't livin'
under the same roof with no nigger." And then he'd tell another of the boarders, and so on and on, and all of sudden
Mary Kay wouldn't have any boarders left.

So it was her secret, one she'd learned by reading the il-
literate letters Mr. Jaffer was always getting from someplace
called Bayou Bay, Louisiana. Letters always saying how
happy his mother was that he was "passing" and she was
glad as how at least one of her "chillun" (that was the word
she used, *chillun*) was "making something of hisself" (another phrase she used) unlike his six brothers and sisters,
two of whom were already dead by age twenty, and two of
whom were in white man's prison in Georgia, she "tole them
not to go to Georgia."

Mary Kay liked to taunt her boarders, but subtly. For instance, to Mr. Parkhurst, who had served time in prison but
never divulged it, she'd said over coffee, "Did you read that
story in the paper about how easy those convicts have it in
the state prison? Why, I think they should flog those fellows,
don't you? And I mean flog them. With a whip." And to the
secret colored man, she'd said, "Have you noticed how up-
pity the coloreds have gotten since the war? I think they're
about the dirtiest, dumbest people on this earth, don't you?"

They looked stunned. And suspicious. And trapped. She could read what they were thinking in their eyes. Did she know? How could she know? Or was this an innocent statement on her part, and they were just reacting out of their guilt? She didn't strike people as sly or cunning. Or mean. But maybe she—but no. She was the landlady. She didn't know. She'd just made a stray remark. Nothing more. But on the other hand, she *did* seem to be speaking directly to them without letting on—

And this morning, watching him polish off the sizable late breakfast, she said to handsome Mr. Robert Langley, "I just can't believe a man as good-looking as you doesn't have a beau, Mr. Langley."

Clean autumn air came through the dining room windows, stirring the lace curtains, pleasing Dulcy, the tabby cat on the windowsill, no end.

Mr. Langley had a long, angular, intriguing face. Black Irisher, he was. Long, dark hair; intense black eyes; and a smile not at all innocent of cruelty.

"Perhaps you'd like to be my beau, Mrs. Washburn."

She laughed, flushed. "Is that a proposal, Mr. Langley?"

"It's a little early in the morning for a proposal like that, I'm afraid."

She hadn't unnerved him. He'd been too slick for her. Mr. Langley was always slick. He never ran out of words, and slick words at that.

She decided to try again to rattle him. "Though I know you've had a lady friend at least once since you've been in town."

He finished cutting the last of his sausage. Didn't look up from his plate. Said, "Oh? And how would you know a thing like that, Mrs. Washburn?"

"One night I couldn't sleep, and I got up to go downstairs, and when I reached the landing, looked out into the backyard—there was a full moon that night, and you could see everything—and there you were with a lady friend."

He brought the piece of sausage to his lips and then paused. "Are you sure it was me?"

"Oh, quite sure, Mr. Langley."

This was fun. She'd rattled him. It was like an especially fun parlor game.

He watched her more closely now with those hard, black, mysterious eyes. "And the woman. Did you recognize her?"

She could have blurted the name out. Of course, she'd recognized her. But teasing people, prolonging the suspense, that was the fun in an enterprise like this one. "I don't guess I did."

"But you said there was a full moon." Cool, just slightly contemptuous voice. The same voice he always used with Mrs. Washburn.

"That's true."

"And you said that you were able to see everything."

"Yes, I guess I did say that, didn't I?"

"But you couldn't see who she was?"

"I guess not."

"Odd," he said and finally put the piece of sausage to his mouth.

She let him eat, sip his coffee. Grandfather clock. A passing cart. Groans and snaps and creaks—the inexplicable noises a house makes.

And Mr. Langley polishing off his breakfast.

And her waiting for exactly the time to say it for maximum impact.

Sipping the last of his coffee.

"Anything else I can get you, Mr. Langley?"

"No, thanks. A fine meal as always."

"Thank you."

"You run a nice place here, Mrs. Washburn."

"Why, thank you again, Mr. Langley. Nothing pleases me more than pleasing my boarders."

Pushing his chair back. Making ready to stand up. To leave.

And her saying, quite idly, just table chatter, "She always complimented me on my house, too."

"She? I guess I don't know who you're talking about."

The moment at last. Saying the name. Watching his face.

"Mrs. Tully. The marshal's wife who was murdered shortly after you came here."

*The woman I saw you kissing in my backyard that night of the full moon. What did she do, Mr. Langley, sneak out of the house when, her husband was asleep? Or maybe he was out of town doing some marshal work. That would be easier, wouldn't it, Mr. Langley, you two sneaking around when he was out of town? Ever so much easier if he was out of town.*

The look of panic—of recognition of the game she was playing, of sneaking in Kate Tully's name only after first mentioning seeing him in the backyard—lasted only a moment. Trapped-animal look. Caught. Then it was gone. And the familiar contempt and amusement was back in his glistening, dark eyes.

"I hear she was a very nice woman."

"Oh, yes. Very nice, Mr. Langley."

"And I also hear good things about her husband."

"I've never cared for him much. A little too standoffish for my tastes."

"Maybe he's shy."

"I've never believed in shyness. I believe that shy people just *say* they're shy, just so they don't actually have to talk to anybody."

The contempt was on the mouth now. A full, chill smile. "Very interesting idea, Mrs. Langley, that there aren't any shy people."

He pushed back. Stood up. "Thanks again for such an excellent meal."

"I appreciate you appreciating it."

"I most certainly do." He looked toward Dulcy enjoying herself sleeping in front of the open window. "Lovely day for a walk. Think I'll head downtown."

"I'm not sure what I'll do," she said, almost to herself.

"I've got an idea."

"You do?"

"Yes." The smile again. Pure mischief now in both eyes and smile. "Why don't you go somewhere you and your dear friend Kate Tully used to go? Enjoy some pleasant memories." He nodded in her direction. "Good day, Mrs. Langley."

And he left the parlor.

During the course of the day, Tully managed to stop into the café three times. They were used to seeing him once, usually for lunch, but three times was an awful lot. Way he looked around, it was clear he was looking for somebody. He described the man he'd seen last night—the man he'd suspected had dropped the locket in his jacket pocket—but none of the employees he talked to recognized the man. He kept dropping back in hopes the man might just pop in for a cup of coffee. No luck.

He also visited all four hotels. No luck there, either, though an overeager clerk thought that there might be just such a man in room 2-B. Tully went up there and knocked. The man who came to the door was short, balding, and had a prominent mole on his left cheek. All Tully said was, "Excuse me, I have the wrong room."

There were six major boardinghouses in town. He saved them for last. They would be the most difficult because the women who ran them would insist he have a piece of pie or cake or at the very least a cookie. Garrulous women ran these places, and they would not let him escape without adding a few pounds. He didn't need help with that. He was putting on a little weight all on his own.

The first three houses were pie-cake-pie, coffee-coffee-sarsaparilla. Between all the sugar and caffeine, he was brain-fried, and he didn't learn a damned thing except that if he decided to put his cottage up for sale and move into town, any of the three landladies would be proud to have him as a permanent boarder. He supposed there was a certain prestige, having the marshal as a resident.

Cake-pie, coffee-coffee was the order of things at the next two boardinghouses. The first of the landladies allowed as how the man sounded sort of familiar except that the man she was thinking of was walleyed. "Was this man by any chance walleyed, Marshal?" The second of the landladies said that she'd had such a boarder awhile back but that he was killed in a train accident up to Stone Junction a couple of months earlier. Probably wasn't him.

Then he came to the flirtatious and amorous Mary Kay Washburn. If you could take college courses in eye-batting and sexual innuendo, Mary Kay would've graduated with honors. First in her class.

Actually, he felt sorry for her. She was one of those women who'd been flattered all her life on her looks. They were nothing special by big-city standards, but in a smaller town, the buxom figure and coy face made more than one man have thoughts his wife would not approve of. But her years were threadbare now, and her winsome, eager flirtiness more pathetic than stimulating.

They sat in her kitchen. He worked on his rhubarb pie— "Just a tiny slice is all, if you please, Mrs. Washburn"—and coffee.

"I might have had a boarder *like* him."

"How long ago?"

"Oh, a couple weeks ago."

"What happened to him?"

"Just up and left, Marshal. You know how they do. Men like secrets." She smiled. "How's the pie?"

"Fine." He'd had so many sweets, he was afraid he was going to break out in pimples. He'd had some acne as a boy. He'd never forgotten it. "He tell you much about what he was doing in town?"

"No, like I say, he kept to himself."

"When did you first start renting to him?"

"I could look it up in my ledger."

"Just approximately."

"Oh, he was probably here three weeks."

"He say that he'd just gotten to town?"

"He didn't say so. But he acted like it."

"Meaning what?"

"Asking directions, things like that. If he'd have been here a while, he wouldn't have asked me about the places he did."

"He have many visitors?"

"None that I can think of."

"He drink much? Gamble?"

"You're really interested in this fella. He must've done something really bad." She sounded purely delighted at the prospect. "But no, he didn't drink so's you'd notice, and if he gambled, he never talked about it."

"Was he bad-tempered?"

"Not at all. A real gentleman. City man, you know. Polished. Good table manners. Talked real nice."

"He make friends with any of the other boarders?"

"No. And they didn't like that, either. Most nights the boarders sit on the front porch and talk. Get to know each other. Have a little beer and do a little smoking. I don't allow smoking in their rooms. Too much risk of a fire."

"Was his rent paid up when he left?"

"Yes. And he left the room in real good shape, too. Not all of them do when they rush off like that."

"And you haven't heard from him since?"

"No, afraid I haven't, Marshal."

"I'd appreciate you letting me know if you see him again."

"I doubt he'll come back. They never do."

"I don't mean just here. Anywhere. The street. The store. Anywhere. If I'm not in the office, just leave word where you saw him."

"You sure do want to find this fella, don't you?"

"Yeah," he said, thinking of the locket. "Yeah, I sure do."

Gretchen, the middle girl, the nine-year-old, Mack Byrnes's favorite child if you absolutely forced him to chose one, was sick with a bad cold, and so when he was in the pharmacy, he found a book she'd like, her favorite kind with a beautiful princess and a handsome prince and a dragon, and so in addition to the medicine he bought for her, he took the book, too.

Gretchen was sleeping when he got home just before noon. Susan was washing laundry down to the crick and then bringing it up to hang out back of their small house. He watched her through the open back door. Five kids had made an old woman of her before her time. All the joy and fun that had once sparkled in her blue eyes had dulled now, and when he suggested anything that didn't fit into her work schedule—going for a walk, taking in a show, making love—she said, "All right, but we'll have to do it fast." And all she did was force herself through whatever activity he'd proposed. It was no fun for her—she was just being dutiful—and thus it was no fun for him, either. He'd even started pitching in with the household chores. But she seemed to resent it. Housekeeping and child rearing were her province and obsession, and she didn't want anybody else poking into her business.

And something else had happened, too.

Three, four months ago.

He suspected what it was, but he tried not to think about it.

That photograph, of course.

God, he'd taken it without even thinking. Just saw it mixed in with a stack of papers and picked it up and put it in his pocket and brought it home.

His pocket. That's where she'd found it. She'd picked up his shirt because it was dirty and needed washing and that was when she saw the picture.

Not that she'd said anything. Never would. Not that kind of woman. If she had pain, she kept it to herself. The doctor said he'd never seen a woman go through childbirth so quietly. You could see that it was damned near killing her—everything seemed to damned near kill her—but she came from stock where any complaining was a sign of weakness. You could pound a railroad spike in her eye, and she probably wouldn't even cry out.

This was worse than a railroad spike.

This was the picture.

And there could be only one possible explanation for it.

And after all she'd scrubbed and cooked and cleaned and

mothered for him, then he went and did something like steal that picture.

He wished he still wanted her and that she still wanted him.

They'd become two strangers.

He wished he still wanted her and that she still wanted him and that late at night they'd make love the way they once did in the moonlight in their Shaker-style bed. God, they'd loved each other so much back then.

He went in and kissed Gretchen on her sweat-damp forehead. This cold was bad one. He could hear it rumbling in her little sparrow chest. God, he loved her. He set the book he'd bought her on the foot of her bed. Then he went out and set the medicine on the kitchen table so Susan would be sure to see it. He supposed he should go to the open door and let her know he was home. But they had so little to say to each other anymore. It was a struggle, and sometimes downright embarrassing.

Then he was out the front door and headed back to town. He was thankful for his job as senior day deputy. It gave him plenty of excuses to stay away from home.

# SIX

ON THE WAY over to Mary Kay Washburn's place, Tully ran into Susan and Delia. His deputy's wife and eldest daughter looked as fresh and clean as the day itself.

"Now's a good time to set up our next appointment," Susan said.

"Appointment?"

"For cleaning your cottage."

"Oh, right."

"How about tomorrow after school?" Delia said. "I'll stop on my way. I'll even pick some fresh flowers for you like last time."

"If I didn't know better," Susan said with a certain air of mischief, "I might think this young girl has taken a fancy to you."

Both Tully and Delia laughed. And blushed.

"Tomorrow afternoon is fine," Tully said, gave them a little salute, and hurried away. He'd been thinking the same thing about the way Delia looked at him sometimes. *Harmless crush; harmless mooning. Sweet, too*, he thought. *Very sweet.*

• • •

Tully had just reached the sidewalk in front of Mary Kay Washburn's boardinghouse when he saw the man at the far end of the block.

Even though the man had his head down, Tully knew immediately this was the same man he'd seen in the café. The one who'd dropped the locket in his jacket pocket.

Tully also knew immediately that the Washburn woman had been lying to him. The man was carrying collars from the Chinese laundry. He wouldn't be on this block with freshly cleaned collars unless he lived here.

But why would Mrs. Washburn lie to Tully?

The first thing was to get out of the way, hide somewhere, not exactly easy with the boardwalk filled with tots playing a variety of games, everything from skip rope to marbles. The temperature was in the low fifties. Perfect for outdoors fun. Every once in awhile, as now, Tully thought of how good it would have been to have had kids with Kate. His own son or daughter. One more reason to mourn her and the life he'd had with her.

He walked quickly down the block, stepped behind a tree.

A chunky boy, probably seven or eight, wore a band with a feather sticking up in it.

Tully peeked around the tree. The man was just now reaching Mary Kay Washburn's house.

"How come you're hiding, Marshal?" the kid wanted to know.

"I'm not hiding."

"You're behind the tree, ain't ya?"

"Yeah, I guess I am."

"Well, ain't that hidin'?"

"Yes, I guess you're right. Now how about bein' quiet?"

"They have to be quiet, too?"

"Who?" Tully said, and soon had his answer as a small group of kids, some dressed as Indians, some as cavalry officers (the yellow kerchiefs gave them away), swarmed around him.

And it was then that the man, halfway up Mrs. Washburn's front steps, noticed the commotion a quarter block away, and looked in Tully's direction.

Tully jerked himself behind the tree.

Had the man seen him? Or had he only seen the kids?

"You gonna kill somebody, Marshal?" one of the freckled cavalrymen asked.

"Probably not today."

"Tomorrow, then?"

"Probably not. I actually don't like killing people."

"If I was marshal, I'd kill people all the time."

A kid like this could give a man second thoughts about having a kid.

"Run along now, boys."

"Have you *ever* killed anybody?" a kid with a pug nose asked.

"No."

"Then how'd you get to be marshal?"

"Did you hear what I said? Run along. And I damn sure mean it."

The *damn* did it. They knew he wasn't kidding.

They looked sullen, angry, disappointed. Here was a lawman who had not only never killed anybody, he didn't seem especially *interested* in killing anybody. What kind of lawman was that? Nobody'd ever write a yellowback about him, that was for sure.

They finally left.

The man was inside the house now.

Tully moved fast. Down the block to Mrs. Washburn's. Up the front steps. And straight inside. No knocking. He just turned the doorknob and went inside.

Parlor, empty. Dining room, empty. No voices coming down the staircase. He headed for the kitchen.

She was wiping down a cut-glass bowl when he barged in.

"Where is he?"

"I didn't hear you knock."

"You lied to me. Now where is he?"

"If you mean Mr. Langley, he's upstairs."

"You tell him I was here?"

She smiled. "I might've mentioned it, I guess."

"Why'd you lie to me?"

"I wasn't sure it was Mr. Langley, and I didn't want to get him in any trouble."

"He have a gun?"

"He carries a Navy Colt, if I'm not mistaken, Marshal."

He thought of several names to call her, if he'd been that sort, then turned and went back to the hall that ran down the center of the house.

The stairs were old wood, and noisy. He had an image of a man waiting for him just out of sight on the second floor, gun drawn. On one step, he tripped and felt vastly foolish and incompetent.

He went up carefully after that, hand on the banister as he moved. His Colt .45 was in his other hand. The landing was empty. Six rooms, three on either side of the landing. All the doors were closed but one. The far one to the right.

He started down that way when a male voice behind him said, "If you're looking for me, Marshal, I'm back here. And you can put that gun away. You won't need it with me."

There was a cold amusement—an arrogance—in the man's voice that Tully didn't like. A superiority. Tully wasn't educated, rich, or fashionable. He wasn't particularly intelligent, virtuous, or cunning. When people talked down to him, the way this man did, he secretly felt he deserved it.

He turned. Langley was his man, all right. Tall, good-looking, just a wee bit of a dandy, at least for these parts. Black Irisher from the looks of him, the Spanish blood dominant. He held a closed straight razor in one hand and a towel in the other. "I was just about to shave, but then I saw you coming up the stairs with your gun drawn and I thought I'd better see what it was all about. Then, when you tripped, I realized you probably weren't as fierce as you looked." He was enjoying himself.

Tully put his gun away.

"You put something in my sheepskin jacket last night," he said.

"I did?"

"Yes . . . this." He took out the locket and held it out for Langley to look at. He flipped it open.

"Well, I'll be damned," Langley said.

"What?"

"That's Kate's old locket."

"You should know. You put it in my pocket. And I want to know why."

"But I didn't put it in your pocket, Marshal. Hell, I haven't seen that thing since the day we split up ten years ago back in St. Louis. I gave it to her for her birthday."

"You must've known her pretty well."

"Known her pretty well?" Langley laughed, and the laugh seemed genuine. "Why, I guess so. She was my wife."

"What the hell are you talking about?" Kate had never mentioned a previous husband.

"That's why I came to town here. She'd never gotten the divorce like she said she would. And I want to get married again." The dark eyes glistened with amusement again. "She wasn't really your wife, Marshal, I'm afraid. She was still married to me."

# PART TWO

Whenever Frank Donnelly wanted to shock somebody—and he got in that kind of mood sometimes when he'd been drinking—he told them about this one particular asylum his brother had him carted off to. Place was so bad he still had nightmares about it.

One of the theories in this place was that if you made the patient associate his perversion with something terrible, he'd stop performing his perversion.

And there was this one guy this one time who always liked to set fire to things. He'd burned down a saloon one night, killing a bunch of people that had made fun of him, his kin had enough money to get him away from Baltimore before the gendarmes could find him. And so one day in this asylum, see, the guards, they caught this bird with some stick matches (which were contraband there and considered a lethal weapon) and you know what they did to him?

Right in front of everybody on the second floor.

They made him take a crap on the floor. That was first of all.

And second of all, they made him eat it.

His own crap.

Can you imagine that? Eating your own crap? Or any
body else's crap, for that matter?

And in front of a bunch of people?

Frank didn't have that particular problem. Didn't want to
set fires. Didn't want to set fires. Didn't want to stab hi
dear, sweet mommy. Didn't want to have sex with othe
men. Didn't want to rape women.

No, all Frank wanted to do was inflict burns, scars, dents
lesions, holes, and indentations on himself.

Now, to Frank, this had always been his own business
He'd made this argument many times to his brother Ralph.

"It's not like I'm hurting anybody, Ralph. And I don'
make you watch me do it or anything. And when I'm in you
casino, I pretty much behave myself, don't I?

"I don't know why they can't leave a feller alone. I reall
don't.

"I never should told you about the nail. That's what did it
That's what you're afraid I'll do, isn't it? That I'll try it wit
the nail."

Guy Frank met a couple years back, he'd done it to him
self with a nail. And showed it to Frank. Right there in th
palm of the guy's hand was the wound. Looked like Christ'
wound. You know, in the hand, when they crucified Him.

These are the thoughts Frank had when he was about 49.
percent awake. The hangover would be an inferno, and hi
bladder would be pained with piss.

But Frank lied to himself all the time, just as he'd lied t
himself just now.

The fact was, he did hurt other people.

This would be when Frank was 61.3 percent awake and
thinking of himself as the Other Frank, the Bad Frank, lik
having a really shitty first cousin who looks just like you bu
does stuff you'd never *think* of doing.

The Bad Frank had killed three women, and Good Ralph
had to pay off lawmen to spare him from the gallows.

Frank was never sure where the Bad Frank came from. H
just showed up from time to time, and when he did . .
When he did . . . brother, watch out.

Now Frank was 83.4 percent awake and thinking about the Tully woman.

The facts are these:

Yes, he did follow her home on several occasions. Never did anything. Just followed her home.

Yes, he did want her most sorely. He wasn't a ladies' man—despite his good looks—but those women he did want he'd be beside himself until he got them.

No, he couldn't remember where he was around the time of her murder.

Yes, he did come home late with his clothes all bloody.

And—he remembered killing her.

Or did he?

He wanted to be careful of that. One of the loony bins he was in, they said that between his drinking and his fantasies, he might think he'd done something that he actually hadn't. He got that way about dreams, too. He'd dream something and then be sure, in the light of day, that he actually did it.

But his bloody clothes were there in the morning. Right next to his bed.

And she *had* been murdered.

And he could sort of remember going out there. . . .

And

and and and and and

And he was now 99.9 percent awake.

And there was no longer any detachment, any irony, any dreamlike sense of the protection Good Ralph afforded him.

There was just the pain and confusion and panic and fear he had known most of his life . . . and now the weeping (that's the only proper word for it) the fucking weeping that so often commenced his day.

He did kill her, the Tully woman.

He was sure of it.

And he was thinking of the nail.

Of the luxuriant pain.

Of the handsome wound.

The nail.

# ONE

RALPH DONNELLY ALWAYS went to the bank on Thursday mornings. He was a man of habits. He was like a postman. Neither rain, sleet, snow, etc. His jaunts from wherever he parked his buggy to the bank rarely held any surprises for him. He did a lot of hat-doffing and a lot of smiling and a lot of baby-kissing. He might have been mistaken for a politician.

Today, however, there was a surprise, and an unpleasant one.

There he was on the boardwalk, chatting with the mother of a sweet little girl in the baby carriage, when he glanced up and saw Father Flaherty walking toward him. He could see that the old man was glowering at him even from this distance.

The priest suffered from rheumatism, arthritis, a chronically sprained ankle, failing vision, and terrible bouts of gout. He rarely left the rectory. And yet here he was on the boardwalk this morning in his priestly black suit and the black thorny cane from the old country pounding on ahead of him like an outsider.

Donnelly's first instinct was to say a quick good-bye to

the woman and her babe, turn around, and flee in the opposite direction. He hadn't talked to the old man since the priest had given him hell in the rectory following confession that day. Holy hell, it had been, too. All about how God expected us to be good citizens and that meant turning in murderers.

Donnelly started to turn away, but that was when the woman thrust little Brenda in his face and said, "Isn't that sweet, Mr. Donnelly? She wants you to kiss her."

Well, maybe she did and maybe she didn't. Because when Donnelly—all this happened in a blur—touched his face to the tiny infant writhing inside her sweet, wrinkled little dress, she didn't give him a kiss at all. She spat up on him. All over his nice new cravat, in fact.

"Oh, my Lord!" said the embarrassed lady and glared at her child. "Look what you've done to poor Mr. Donnelly, Brenda! Just look what you've done!" As if the child understood. Or cared.

"It's fine, Mrs. Chauncy. I'll just wipe it off when I get to my office."

He was hardly paying attention. He stood transfixed, watching the old priest descend upon him like a stormy messenger from God on high.

"Oh, let me get it for you, please!" She said.

"No, I'm afraid I'm already late. I'll see you later, Mrs. Chauncy."

Retreat. Flight. The only answer when the priest was closing in this way. But even as he turned, he could hear the cane pound harder, faster against the boardwalk. How could a man that old and infirm possibly move that fast?

He started to walk away. The Chauncy woman was still pleading to his back about letting her wipe the baby puke off his fine new cravat. And the cane was pounding harder, faster—

"Donnelly! Ralph Donnelly! You stop right there and wait for me!"

It was like having the nun call you out on the playground.

You froze, terrified and humiliated to be singled out this way, especially with everybody looking.

And everybody *was* looking.

All along the boardwalk, cowboys, merchants, ladies with children, ladies without children, ladies with hats, ladies without hats, ladies with bustles, ladies without bustles, drunks, Indians, soldiers—everybody turned to stare at the object of Father Flaherty's wrath.

And they stared with some amusement, too.

Who else in town would dare speak in such a tone to Ralph Donnelly? Not even the mayor; not even Ben Tully. And if it had been one of the other priests, the younger ones, Donnelly would have demanded that Flaherty get rid of him.

But this was Flaherty himself.

The priest smelled of sweat, whiskey, and myriad lotions rubbed on old flesh to rob it of pain. Stuff the Monkey Ward and Sears catalogs sold by the trainload.

Flaherty hobbled up to him. "I haven't seen you at Mass."

"I've been busy, Father."

"You've been avoiding me."

Donnelly glanced around, hoping nobody was listening. The priest had at least lowered his voice. How could eyes this red, rheumy, and half blind be intimidating? And yet somehow, they were.

"And you know *why* you've been avoiding me."

"I just made a mistake was all. What I told you in confession, I mean."

"You're just making things worse. And you know it."

Despite his bluster, there was a certain old-man sweetness that seemed to lie beneath it. As if he actually cared for Donnelly and cared *about* him. Soul-wise, that is.

"It'll always be on your conscience and on your soul."

"I told you, Father. I made a mistake."

"A mistake. Don't insult me any more with such a stupid lie."

"He didn't kill her. He really didn't."

"I take it by that you mean your brother."

Donnelly's eyes got frantic again. Was anybody listening?

The priest had lowered his voice even more, thank goodness.

"They hung the right man, Father. They really did."

"I don't believe that."

"Why not? They found him with blood all over him and all sorts of things of hers from the house in his pockets."

"He told the men who hung him that they came upon the body, Ralph. And she was already dead."

"Why would you believe him?"

"It's just a feeling I have." He paused. "And the fact that you didn't stop them from lynching him."

Donnelly felt his cheeks grow hot.

"Mack Byrnes begged you to help him. And usually you would have. You want people to think the best of you, Ralph. You want to be respectable. And you want Pine City to be respectable. And that means no lynching. You want people to think better of us than that—that we're not just another lawless frontier town. But you didn't stop the lynching. Wouldn't get involved. Which means you had a secret reason for the lynching to happen."

As much as Donnelly wanted to pull away from the man, he couldn't. Even speaking in little more than a whisper, the shaggy old sod was a powerful force that drew you in.

"And you know what that secret reason was. And so do I. An innocent man died that night, Ralph, and you know it. And his blood is on your soul. You killed him sure as you slapped the horse yourself. And you think you know who the real killer is."

"He didn't do it, Father. He really didn't."

"You know better than that. And so do I." He swung his cane wide, as if to sweep Donnelly off the boardwalk. "Now, get out of my way. I can't take the sight of you any longer."

And then he was gone, moving again with surprising speed down the boardwalk.

Donnelly became self-conscious. He had a sense—a nightmare dread—that he was standing naked on the apron of a stage and thousands of people were watching him.

But he was surprised to find that nobody was watching him. Once the priest had lowered his voice, people lost interest. Casual conversations held no fascination for them.

He took a deep breath. He would go on about his business. He would continue strolling down the boardwalk. He would smile a magnificent, good-citizen smile, and hat-doff and baby-kiss, and he wouldn't think even once about the possibility that his brother was a killer. Not even once would he think about it.

He was very close to the bank before he glanced down and saw the baby's vomit on his cravat.

"It's probably not anything you want to hear, Tully."

They were in the café, Tully and this Robert Langley, coffee in front of each of them, Langley seasoning his with a bit of bourbon from a silver flask.

Getting crowded now, counter and tables alike, the lunch folks drifting in.

"She was my wife, Langley. I want to know the truth about her."

"Well," Langley said, the contempt still in his voice and eyes, "she was *my* wife, too. And I don't mean to defame her now that she's dead."

"Did you see her when you came back here?"

Langley looked right at him and said, "Now what do you think, Marshal? You want me to say no and spare your feelings? Of course, I saw her. I came here to get her to sign divorce papers."

"You know what I'm asking."

A harsh laugh. "You're almost making me feel sorry for you, Marshal. And I'll tell you, if there's one type of man I don't like to feel sorry for, it's one who wears a badge." He paused. He was having fun. "What you're asking is, did we sneak off and have a roll in the hay?"

Which was what Tully wanted to know indeed. But didn't have nerve enough to give voice to. He just sat there, awaiting the dreaded word.

"We came close a couple of times. She was a passionate

woman, as I'm sure you know. But for the record, she pulled back the times we got together. Said it wasn't right. Said that even though she didn't love you, she respected you and owed you being faithful. I'm afraid she was still in love with me, Marshal."

"I don't believe you."

"You don't *want* to believe me. But I think you know the truth when you hear it. And you just heard it. I'm surprised Mrs. Washburn didn't tell you about the times she saw Kate in the backyard with me. Kate snuck down to see me a couple of times when you were gone overnight on business. We put on quite a show for that gossipy old bitch Mrs. Washburn."

Tully's face was scalded with rage, shame, despair. He couldn't let himself believe this stranger's words, and yet he had to admit to himself that the words could be true. Kate had always been mysterious about her past.

"Tell me about you two."

"Haven't had enough yet, Marshal? I guess you're a man who likes punishment. But why don't I spare you?"

Tully's voice was low as a growl. "Tell me right here and right now, you sonofabitch, or I swear I'll take you outside and kill you with my hands."

But Langley wasn't impressed with Tully's anger. "That's more like it, Tully. Take me back to your jail and beat me up. And when you get tired of doing it, have one of your deputies come in and take over for you. That's what you law boys wear the badge for, isn't it? So you can beat up people and maybe even kill them and get away with it. You're a bunch of punks is all. Just a bunch of punks."

"How many times you been in prison, Langley?"

"What's that supposed to mean?"

"It means you talk like a convict who's run into a bad lawman here and there. You don't get that anger any other way." They were in a booth at the back at the café. Hard for anybody to see them. Tully said, "You want me to treat you like those other lawmen did, fine, I'll be happy to oblige you. I even know of a couple little tricks they use in Mexico a lot.

So right now you tell me about you and Kate, or I take you over to the jail and we start having some fun together. Now, which is it going to be?"

Apparently, this time Langley understood just how much Tully loathed him and would be willing to do whatever was necessary to find out about Kate.

Langley even gave Tully the satisfaction of shuddering a little.

Langley sighed and then said, "First of all, her real name wasn't Kate."

And then he proceeded to tell his story.

Just his luck to get one who smelled bad.

You'd think a hobo wouldn't especially care if his traveling companion didn't exactly exude an odor of cleanliness. But Bert Lawson had always been particular about who he traveled with. Francis Xavier was a good example. No matter how bad things got on the road, Francis Xavier always managed to bathe and shave regular.

Which was a lot more than you could say about the portly Deputy Jim Van Amburg sitting next to him in the train seat. The man had sweated his suit coat so bad, the armpits were rimed with white acids from his body. His long, black hair wasn't any better. He had some kind of rash that ringed the front of his hairline and showed up again around the lobes of his ears on the jawline. But the man's breath was the worst thing of all. Whoo boy. That man had probably not tended to his teeth since he was in the Civil War.

They were handcuffed together.

"You don't try no funny stuff," the deputy—or *deppity* as he called himself—said as the engine several cars ahead started up.

"Now what kinda funny stuff could I try exactly?" Lawson said, nodding to the handcuff.

"I've known men to try it."

"Well, not this man."

"That's just what they said," the deppity said, "right before they tried it."

It was gonna be one long sumbitch of a ride to Pine City.

They started out as pickpockets and worked their way into other, more profitable kinds of criminal activities such as passing counterfeit money, housebreaking, forgery, and swindling.

They did all this in Midwestern cities such as St. Louis, where they'd both grown up and met, and Cleveland and Chicago. Both served brief prison sentences. They always worked as a team and always relied on her looks and quiet manner as their best weapon. Who could suspect that such a pretty, gentle woman could be a grifter? But grifter she was, and so was he.

When he was twenty-four, he gave the stage a try. He was good at it. Not New York good, maybe, but What Cheer, Iowa, and Midlothian, Illinois, and Paducah, Kentucky, good at it. He was the star of a traveling show that performed ham theater for yokels, usually in tents. While he was performing, she worked the crowd. Dozens of drunks fell in love with her instantly as she picked their pockets and passed queer currency. He always liked to joke that they'd come by their work "honestly." His father had been a ham actor, and her mother (she'd never known who her father was) was a prostitute and thief.

The first miscarriage changed her. Took a certain vitality from her. She was near death for a time, and there in the grimy free hospital ward, the dying and dead all around her, a gray graveyard of those about to be buried, she began to read newspapers and magazines of other places, other sorts of lives. She didn't want an eyrie, didn't want to be a princess. She just wanted a clean life where you didn't have to fear the police and where you didn't have to prey on the poor, stupid unwashed of the angry city streets.

She told him she wanted them both to head west, start over. He assumed she would be all right once the gloom of her miscarriage lifted. When she realized he wouldn't be coming west with her, she cut her wrists right there in the ward. They saved her. He realized how serious she was and didn't know what to do. She was his wife by this time and in his faithless way, he loved her. They'd been together since they were twelve years old. How could you end such a relationship? She was lover, sister, mother, friend, accomplice.

"So I just told her that I just couldn't see myself out West and that there wasn't anything to do except split up. Get a divorce. I was afraid she might try to kill herself again. You probably don't believe it, but I really did care about her." Langley cleared his throat. "But she took it much better than I would've thought. I think everything put together—you know, the miscarriage and her plans to go west and then her suicide attempt—I think she was just kind of dazed. She said she'd give me the divorce. I was going back on the road—our little traveling show was pretty popular in the sticks—and I asked her if she'd take care of the divorce. That was pretty stupid, when you think about it. Putting her in charge of a divorce she didn't want. But I didn't worry about it too much at the time. The idea of getting married again was pretty remote. I just didn't like being tied down, period. So I went back on the road and forgot about it. Then, about a year ago, I met this lady on a riverboat—they're dying out, but they still book a few theatrical shows like ours—and I decided it was time for me to settle down."

"So you went looking for Kate."

"I still can't get used to calling her Kate. But yes, looking for Kate."

"And you found her."

"And I found her. Finally. It wasn't easy."

"And she wouldn't give you a divorce, and you had an argument, and you killed her."

The lizard smile. "Now wouldn't that make it nice and simple for our favorite lawman?"

"So you're denying it?"

"Of course I'm denying it."

"Did she say she'd give you a divorce?"

He splayed big hands on the table of the booth they were sitting in. He looked down at them so he wouldn't have to meet Tully's eyes. "I'll have to hurt you again, Marshal."

"You're going to tell me she wanted to run away with you?"

Langley looked up. "Pretty close. She said she needed a month to explain things to you, to make you see that while she cared for you, she was still in love with me."

"If she wasn't in love with me, then why she did she want to have a baby so bad?"

Langley seemed surprised. "Because having a baby meant more to her than anything else in the world."

Tully thought of her face, there in the terrible dawn shadows of her miscarriage. Her gaunt face and tears, and then the long days and nights of her making no sound at all, lying in bed, sleeping as often as possible.

"I guess you're right about that, Langley."

"So we shouldn't be enemies. You loved her, and I loved her."

"You figure that's how things work, huh? You loved her so much you ran out on her."

"That doesn't mean I didn't love her." He tapped his chest. "In here."

Tully wondered how many times Langley had used those words and that gesture on stage. He did it so smoothly it was devoid of meaning.

"And why do you want *me* for the killer, Marshal? They hanged the killer. That big bastard. Conners, or whatever his name was. That hobo."

"Maybe he didn't do it."

"You trying to tell me your nice little town here may have hanged the wrong man?" He seemed delighted. "Now, that would make a nice news story, wouldn't it?" He considered his words for a moment. "But they found blood on him."

"I know."

"And things from your house."

Tully nodded. "That kind of evidence isn't always conclusive."

"It sure sounds conclusive to me. And it sure strikes me funny—if you loved her as much as you say—that you aren't grateful to the men who hanged him. You know who they were, by the way?"

"I've got a pretty good idea."

"Maybe you should toss them a party."

"I don't toss parties for lynch mobs."

"Not even when they lynched the killer of the woman you say you loved? I'd give 'em a party that'd go all night if I was you."

Now it was Tully's turn to be silent. Sometimes, so many thoughts and feelings crowded your head that you just had to sit and try to calm yourself. Make some sense of them.

He wished he believed Langley here was lying. But he didn't. Langley enjoyed hurting Tully's feelings, but for some reason, everything he said sounded true. He made simple statements, he didn't actor them up the way he might have. The truth was most often plainspoken, not all gussied up. And a lot of what Langley said explained the mysterious holes in Kate's background, the parts she'd never really discussed.

Langley said, "I really did love her, Marshal. Whatever you may think to the contrary."

"You still could've killed her."

"You could've killed her, too."

"I was out of town."

"So you say. But you could've snuck back early and gone to your cottage and killed her."

"You don't really believe that, do you?"

"I know how love works on people, Marshal. Especially when it's love that's not returned. She didn't love you, and I think you knew that all along. You might have done something crazy—something you didn't even plan to do."

"You know better than that."

Langley took his hat and stood up. "Actually, I don't know better than that. If you don't think Conners did it, then that leaves everything open to all sorts of possibilities." He cinched his hat on. "Good day, Marshal."

# TWO

AROUND TWO THAT afternoon, Mack Byrnes came back to Tully's office and said, "Karl Sieversen is here."

"What the hell does he want?"

"He's pissed off about that Conners girl."

Tully set his pen down and flexed his fingers. Arthritis, the family curse, crept through his hands. It would only get worse as he got older. "She doesn't have a right to come here and ask questions?"

"He knows she'll find out the truth."

Sieversen, an erstwhile respectable manufacturer of wagons and wagon parts, had fought on the blue side during the war, just as Tully had. But unlike Tully and most other veterans, he had developed a taste for organizing groups of night raiders along military lines. Sieversen was frustrated that there weren't any more wars to fight. Long before Tully had come to Pine City, Sieversen had led his raiders against Indians and any other group of people he didn't like. He'd also run off two marshals he didn't think were tough enough for the job. He had tested Tully several times and found that Tully was not only tough but smart. He planted spies in Sieversen's night-riding outfit and managed to head off raids before they happened. The "truth" Mack referred to was the fact that it had been Sieversen who'd led Conners's lynching.

Tully said, "Send him in."

"You want me to stay?"

"Sign of weakness. He'll think I'm afraid to see him alone."

Mack laughed. "You're right. That's just how he'd see it, isn't it?"

"He never got over the fact that he was a captain in the army and got to strut around in a fancy uniform. Made him believe he was tough. God, think of all those Fourth of July speeches he gives."

They both laughed. Even little kids headed for the hills when Sieversen climbed the bandstand on the Fourth and began to talk about his "grand, glorious days serving these grand, glorious United States of America." He had once been clocked at one hour and thirty-eight minutes in baking, burning sunlight.

"I'll go get him," Mack said.

"Thanks. But if he starts giving me a speech, I'm climbing right out that window over there."

Mack watched him a moment. "You all right?"

"Yeah. Why?"

"All the jokes. You just don't tell all that many."

"I'm fine." But he wasn't, of course. For seven years he'd wanted to know about Kate. The real Kate. Well, it turned out she wasn't Kate at all but somebody else entirely. A grifter, a sad woman who couldn't bear children, a woman who liked and respected him but didn't love him. Loved another grifter named Langley. So he told jokes in an effort to convince himself he could handle all the pain.

"I'm fine," he said again. But this time he didn't sound quite so certain of it.

"You need to talk or anything, you know I'll be glad to listen."

"I appreciate it, Mack."

Mack Byrnes went and got Sieversen.

• • •

Mary Kay Washburn sat in the parlor pretending to read the
*Ladies' Home Journal*. She wished she wasn't only pretending. She loved the magazine. She liked to dream about living in some of the homes depicted on its pages. Or
surrounding herself with some of the men she saw there. Elegant gentlemen when in society but carnal beasts when in
the bedroom.

But it was difficult to concentrate because she was thinking about her boarder Mr. Langley. Marshal Tully sure
wanted to find him in a bad way. And after they'd met up,
what happened? Was Mr. Langley in jail? And if so, for what
reason?

There had been a slightly sinister air about him when he'd
first appeared on her doorstep one rainy afternoon some
time back. But the sinister air only enhanced the man's out-
size, theatrical good looks. He'd told her he was a stage
actor, and she believed him. The way he moved, the way he
talked, the intimate, almost oppressive way he looked at her
sometimes. Her thighs got weak.

But *slightly sinister* was different from being somebody
the law wanted.

She knew all about criminals. She had two cousins who
were in and out of prison, and she'd been forced, at several
points to travel with her sick aunt to visit them. If there had
ever been any dime-novel romance in her about lawless
men, it was crushed by her prison visits. The shabby, filthy,
surly men she saw peering at her through the bars terrified
her. Easy to imagine them raping and murdering and muti-
lating. And easy to imagine that she was one of their victims.

Now, all she wanted was to get Mr. Langley out of her
boardinghouse.

But what if her request sent him into a murderous frenzy?
Just a few issues ago, the very magazine she held in her
hands warned women about "Five Types of Men to Watch
Out For." At the very top of the list was "The Smooth-Talk-
ing Confidence Man and His Natural Habitats—Trains,
Stagecoaches and Cafés." The article had pointed out that

while most confidence men were not violent, a few had been known to fly into homicidal rages when challenged in any way. Delicately as possible—because the readers were womenfolk of the most delicate tastes—the article went on to hint at a few of the terrible fates that had befallen the victims.

She sat in the bay window. She put the magazine down on her lap. She looked out into the sunny street. Bicycles and unicycles everywhere on such a warm day. She wondered about getting up and making her boarder, Mr. Sims, his cigarettes. She had one of those little rollers that allowed her to produce twenty well-made cigarettes in a short time. He always paid her for her time. Even so, he saved money over ready-mades. Maybe she should occupy her time this way instead of waiting by the window for Mr. Langley.

But she didn't want him to catch her unawares someplace.

She could see herself rolling the cigarettes in the sewing room—she liked it there because of the strong, direct sunlight—and him sneaking into the house and sneaking into the room and—

She sometimes had to set aside her mystery novels because her imagination was so strong it led her to believe that the events in the novel were about to happen to her.

And then he was there.

Crossing the street. Looking—

Well, the brim of his dramatic black hat was so low, she couldn't really see his face.

But even from this distance, she sensed that he was not happy.

She wondered why Marshall Tully was after him.

And then she remembered a mystery story by Louisa Alcott about a dashing man who murdered lovely, elegant women just like Mary Kay Washburn and then dismembered them and put their parts in steamer trunks.

Had Mr. Langley snuck a steamer trunk up to his room without her knowing it?

Then he was there. On the porch. Coming inside. It was just like reading one of her mystery stories: her breath coming in gasps, her forehead fevered with perspiration, her heart a wild fluttering bird in her bosom.

And then he was there.

"I was in the war," Sieversen said.

"I'm well aware of that," Tully said.

"And one thing I learned in the war is how easily morale can be undermined."

"I agree with you there."

"Very, very easily."

"I'm wondering what your point is, Mr. Sieversen."

"My point is that there's a young woman going all over town asking questions about the night that the Conners man was hanged."

"I believe the word is *lynched* Mr. Sieversen."

"*Lynching* leaves a bad taste in my mouth. It implies lawlessness. The man was guilty. There's no doubt about that."

"None at all?"

"Not in my mind."

"I see."

"The state investigator was here, and nobody would cooperate with him, and he went back to the capital with his tail tucked between his legs, and that was that. Or so I thought. But now she's going around and asking the same questions the state investigator did."

Sieversen was stout rather than big. He carried himself with self-conscious decorum. He favored dark suits that were cut in military fashion and severity. He was a balding blond man with whiskey-blotched cheeks and a pugnacious mouth.

"You owe this town for what we did for you."

"Then you're admitting you were part of the lynching?"

Sieversen paused. You could see the calculation in his blue eyes. what sort of legal trouble had he just gotten himself into? "I don't admit anything. I meant 'we' as citizens was all."

"And just what did all of you good citizens do for me?"

"Killed the man who killed your wife. I'd be damned grateful, if I were in your shoes."

"She may be right, you know."

"Who may be right? That girl, you mean?"

"Nan Conners is her name."

"She isn't right, and you damned well know it. She's just here to stir up trouble. And the town council's not going to let her do it." He seemed exasperated. "This can't be good for you, Marshal. Don't you want to put it all behind you? You know we got the right man. Maybe lynching wasn't the best way to handle it—sometimes anger gets ahold of a person and makes them do things they come to regret—but it's a closed chapter. For you and for the whole town. Let's just leave it that way. Let's not have this Nan Conners going all over town and opening it up again."

"You're scared, Sieversen, and I don't blame you. You're scared that maybe you hanged the wrong man. And you were in the lead. That, I don't have any doubt about. Maybe you got the right man, and maybe you didn't. If the girl can turn up some new evidence, I'm obliged to give it a hearing. You and the town council said you wanted a 'professional lawman' when you hired me on. And that's what I'm trying to be. And if you did hang the wrong man, the state inspector's going to come back, and this time he's going to make sure he gets the information he needs."

"You held him off, too, that man from the capital."

Tully sighed, pushed his chair away from the desk. Walked to the window. Looked out on the dusty, crowded street. He was trying to keep his mind on business. He was trying not to think about the things Langley had told him.

"I was wrong to do that," Tully said. "I should've cooperated and helped him."

"Then why the hell didn't you?"

Tully looked away from the window, back to Sieversen. "Because I couldn't think clearly. Too much anger and too much pain. I probably would've lynched him myself, same as you men did. At least, right then I would've. But now that I can see things more clearly . . . You didn't do anybody a favor, you men. What I need and what the law needs is the truth."

"The blood on his hands and the things he stole from your house—"

"Maybe it was just the way he said. You ever think of that, Sieversen? Maybe she really was dead when those two 'bos got there. Maybe they was hiding in the woods by our cottage. Or maybe he was already long gone." He walked back to his desk. "The truth. That's all that matters to the law, and it's all that matters to me."

"I want that woman chased out of this town. The mayor said you agreed to do just that."

"I think I was wrong about that, too. If you hanged the right man, then you'll probably be safe. There's still enough lynch law fever in this state to save you. That's what you men are hoping for. But if you hanged the wrong man—"

"She'll be gone by noon tomorrow, Tully. And if you're not careful, so will you."

Tully shook his head. "We'll just have to wait and see what happens, Sieversen. We've both got a real big stake in this. Yours is a lot bigger than mine, I guess. You could end up on the end of a rope just the way Conners did."

She wondered if he had a knife concealed somewhere. That was how the really bad ones did it. Knives. Not guns. Carving up bloody human meat.

Langley saw Mary Kay Washburn in the parlor, but he didn't acknowledge her in any way. Instead, he walked straight for the staircase and started climbing upstairs.

She decided she might as well get it over with. She'd come up with a convincing lie—at least it was the sort of lie *she* would believe—one that he should accept if he had any kind of soul at all.

She rushed to the bottom of the stairs.

He was nearly to the top when she called his name.

He stopped, turned. "Did you want something, Mrs. Washburn?"

Could she go through with it? What if she was transparent, and he recognized it for the lie it was? She wished she knew why Marshal Tully had wanted to see him. Maybe he wasn't a monster at all. Maybe he was a simple thief or something. Maybe—

"I wanted to tell you about my cousin."

"And why would you want to tell me about your cousin, Mrs. Washburn?"

"Because he's . . . sick."

"Well, that's too bad. But I'm not sure why I'd be interested in hearing about it."

"Because he's sick—he was a miner and he's got terrible breathing problems—and he needs somewhere to stay."

"Ah." A cold smile. "And you're going to tell me he needs to stay here."

"Why, yes." She knew she was blushing.

"And you just hate to ask me to relinquish my room, but you have no choice?"

"Are you making fun of me, Mr. Langley?" She hated being made fun of. Couldn't stop herself from jousting with him.

"No, I just find it strange that the first boarder you'd ask to move is me."

"Why, that's simple enough. You're the newest."

"No, I'm not the newest, Mrs. Washburn. Tom Gleason is."

"Oh. I guess that's right—"

"You want to get rid of me because Marshal Tully came calling."

"No, I—"

The cold smile again. "You're afraid I might be a slasher or something. Isn't that what they called that man in Baltimore, the one who cut up all those women? The Slasher?"

"Mr. Langley, truly I—"

He took off his dramatic hat and half-bowed to her. "I am going to make it easy for you, madame. Tomorrow morning, I'm going to pack all my things and remove myself from your odious old house. I've come into some money, and I plan to stay at a place where I don't have to fight bedbugs

for the sheet every night." He started to turn away, then
glanced back at her. "I do hope your cousin gets better,
madam."

The smirk was perfect, immaculate.

She stood watching the backs of his trousers and the heels
of his boots ascend the steps. He moved with a steady, certain gait; there would always be the mark of the actor about
him. Maybe he lived his life in scenes, the way you did on
stage.

She didn't have to ask what scene this one would be. This
would be where the dashing cad made fun of the middle-
aged woman for the sport of the audience. Audiences loved
scenes like this. This was, in fact, the essence of comedy:
cruelty for the sake of laughter.

Now she was more convinced than ever that he was a
murderer.

And she did not have bedbugs, dammit.

Nan Conners was proud of herself. She had been talking to
people in Pine City for less than four hours, and already a
name had turned up she hadn't heard before: Rafe Simmons.

"That was the first person I thought of when I heard that
Kate Tully had been killed," Pops Boynton said. He was a
white-haired man with a friendly face and a Santa Claus
belly over which was distended an apron that appeared to be
made out of white sailcloth. Pops had owned general stores
all his life, following the gold camps mostly. He was as rest-
less as the miners to move on. Until he reached fifty, anyway. He took a bride, bought land, started going to church
and attending town council meetings to bitch about the
things all the other bitchers bitched about. He was, for the
first time in his life, a regular citizen. He'd owned the general store here in Pine City for nine years now and knew
more gossip than any dozen church ladies you cared to
name.

"So he was in prison?"

"Yep. And Tully put him there."

"And tell me again what he said to you a couple weeks ago."

"He said, and these are his exact words, we was watchin' people in the street, see, and we seen Tully walk by, he said, 'Someday, somebody's gonna give that cocky bastard what he deserves.' Pardon my French, miss."

She liked being in general stores, the smells of spices and leather and candies and tobacco, the sights of abundant groceries and firearms and fresh fabrics in bolts, the potbelly stove working to take the chill off, hardware and dry goods and barrels packed tight with sugar and molasses and flour. As a little girl, she'd had dreams of *living* in a general store with all the dolls and pretty dresses and even the player piano that only the rich folks could afford.

"He say anything more?"

"Oh, just the usual stuff."

"About Tully?"

"Some of it was about Tully. Rafe wanted this land from this widow woman, so he kept tryin' to drive her off. Rafe had land right next to it, and he wanted to expand. She had the better land for grazing. And she had more water. So Rafe started workin' on her, tryin' to scare her. Finally, he got hisself all drunked up one night and set her barn on fire. She couldn't prove who it was, but Tully kept after it and after it 'til two of Rafe's own ranch hands told Tully that Rafe had admitted to them he done it. And he was sober when he admitted it."

"So, he went to prison."

"And sat in there hatin' Tully every day of his sentence."

"He didn't think he should've gone to prison? He broke the law."

Pops Boynton shrugged. "You gotta understand Rafe. He thinks he's a little betters'n everybody else."

"Why's that?"

"Got himself a high school diploma, for one thing. Married the prettiest gal in the valley, for the other. And is a first cousin of the governor."

"The governor couldn't have given him a pardon?"

Pops Boynton grinned with a nice clacking pair of store-boughts. "That's the thing. The governor, he grew up with Rafe. Knows what a bully he is. And a hothead. He helped Rafe outta all kinds of scrapes in the past, but he figured this time he'd teach Rafe a lesson. Let him spend some time in prison. The jury wanted Rafe to spend six years. The governor convinced the parole board to let Rafe out early."

"So Rafe was the first person you thought of when Tully's wife died?"

"You bet. That'd be a pretty good way to pay somebody back, wouldn't it—kill their wife? And then have the satisfaction of seeing somebody else hang for it?"

She had told them she was a journalist from the state capital, not that she was Francis Xavier's sister. "You realize that most people in town think the right man was hanged?"

The store-bought grin again. "Yeah, they think I talk too much, anyway. But the people that crab the worst about me are the ones always sneakin' around askin' me if I got any good gossip. That's how people are. That's what ole Pops has learned all these years of havin' general stores. People are hypocrites. You ever noticed that?"

She laughed. "I'd say I've noticed that every once in a while."

"And cruel."

"Yes, I've noticed that, too."

"And afraid to say what's really on their minds."

"The same way you're afraid to ask me about the scar on my face?"

He flushed. "I guess I have been kinda lookin' at it. Sorry if I hurt yer feelin's."

"Oh, it's natural to be curious."

"You're so pretty and all. And that scar—"

They swept through the door, two of them, and Ralph Donnelly spoke first. "What're you saying to this young woman, Pops?"

"I reckon that's my business."

"I reckon it isn't," Sieversen said. "Not when the welfare of this entire community is at stake, it isn't."

But Pops remained as festive as Santa. "You speaking for the community now, are you, Mr. Sieversen? I kinda thought we left that sort of thing to our elected officials."

Sieversen started to lunge for Pops, but Donnelly put a big, quick hand on his shoulder. Donnelly pulled his friend back and then stepped up to Pops.

"Sieversen always gets a little hot, Pops. I'm sorry," Donnelly said. He nodded to Nan. "You know who she is?"

"Sure. A reporter from the capital."

"Afraid not. She's the sister of the man who got hanged."

"I'll be damned," Pops said. Then he laughed. "I never was able to resist a pretty face."

"She means to start trouble, Pops, for all of us. For this whole town. I know you weren't in favor of the lynching, but I also know that you think we got the right man."

"Unless it was that damned Rafe," Pops said.

"Rafe?" Sieversen snapped. "You only say it's Rafe because he swindled you out of a thousand dollars on a land deal. It was your fault for not checking with somebody from the bank. They would've told you that Rafe was lying about the railroad planning to use that parcel for right-of-way land. You've been laying for Rafe ever since."

Nan could see that Sieversen was telling the truth. Pops looked embarrassed, flustered.

"You say anything about anybody other than Rafe?" Donnelly said.

"Nope."

"You sure?"

"Positive," Pops said, properly chastised now. He didn't seem so large now, or so festive.

"Young lady," Sieversen said, turning to Nan, "we are telling you on behalf of the citizens of Pine City to leave our town on the six-oh-three train this evening. You'll notice that I said we're *telling*. Not asking you. Telling you. Ordering you, if you want it in blunt terms."

Donnelly spoke in gentler words. "What you're doing, miss—and believe me, I sympathize with you, your brother dying that way and all—but what you're doing isn't helping anybody. It's not going to bring your brother back, and it's going to cause you and everybody else misery. The lynching wasn't our finest hour. I'll certainly admit that, and I apologize on behalf of the town. But I think a little ways down the road you'll realize that your brother was the murderer and that justice was done."

"The six-oh-three," Sieversen said. "I'd be at the depot at least half an hour ahead of time to get your ticket."

Again, Donnelly was commiserative. "I'd be happy to buy you a big meal before you go, if you'd like, Miss Conners."

"No, thank you. That's not necessary."

"So then you'll be going for sure?" Sieversen said. He was straining on his leash again, only moments away from bluster and threats and rage.

"I haven't decided yet, I guess," she said. She looked at Pops. "Thanks for the conversation, Pops. I enjoyed it."

She gathered herself, nodded to Donnelly, dismissed Sieversen with a glare, and left the store.

# THREE

ELEVEN MEN HAD participated in the lynching, and ten of them now sat in a room that belonged to a local lodge they were members of. The eleventh man was down with a fever of some kind.

Sieversen had called the meeting, and he was running it. He stood behind a table with a small podium mounted atop it. He was as self-important as ever. If you so much as coughed, sneezed, or—God help you—yawned, you received his glare of glares. God didn't demand this kind of unfettered attention. But then God was only God, and Sieversen was, after all, Sieversen.

He was saying—standing between the American and the state flag, his left hand clutching his lapel the way old Abe Lincoln himself had done it—he was saying, "You all know about the girl. Nan Conners I'm talking about."

General, rumbling agreement. They all knew about Nan Conners.

"And you know why she's here."

More rumbling agreement.

"What amazes me, then, is that you admit you know who

she is and why she's here, but not one of you came to me about her. I had to come to you. I had to call this meeting."

A spectrum of faces—young, middle-aged, a few right on the cusp of real age—watched Sieversen. This was what a lynch mob looked like in light of day: a farmer, three cowhands, a merchant, a stagecoach driver, a blacksmith, a faro operator, an insurance salesman. They were husbands, fathers, uncles, godfathers, not the night riders of dime novels.

None of them looked like criminals, none of them *were*, strictly speaking, criminals. As much as the Eastern papers complained about lynching, it had long held a somewhat respectable place in frontier jurisprudence. Lawmen and judges were not only few and far between in this vast land, they were too often susceptible to bribes and threats.

So local men took it upon themselves to bring law and order to their towns. And sometimes—not nearly as often as the Eastern press would have you believe— mobs took it upon themselves to execute men (and the occasional woman) they felt to be guilty. Most people didn't get too excited about it because the great majority of men who got hanged were outlaws—bank robbers, train robbers, rustlers, rapists, killers—men who had long histories of breaking the law.

And nobody considered the men who hanged them criminals.

Except those in the state's attorney's office.

"Have you thought through what this Nan Conners is trying to do?"

They were being chastised, and they knew it, and they also knew better than to resist in any fashion. When Sieversen got going, he could set old Satan himself to running.

"She's here, in case you gentlemen haven't figured it out yet, to prove that we were wrong. To prove that we hanged the wrong man. To prove that we are, in fact, murderers. And that the state's attorney should be treating us as such. To make things even worse, I spoke with our illustrious town marshal this morning, and he tells me that he's sorry now that he didn't cooperate with the investigator the state's attorney sent out here. Now that he's over the shock of his wife's death, he's beginning to wonder if we hanged the wrong man, too. He called me everything but a killer when I was in his office this morning."

One of the cowhands raised his hand. "This ain't gonna sit well with everybody, but somebody's got to say it. What if we did hang the wrong man?"

"That's the last time I want to hear that spoken by any one of us," Sieversen said.

"Damned right," said the faro dealer. He had three daughters. He didn't want to end up seeing them but once a month in a small, dank prison visitors room.

The merchant, who sold ladies' goods and was the brunt of many jokes questioning his masculinity, not only spoke but stood up. "The man had blood on his hands. The man had things from her house in his pockets. He was drinking and couldn't give a good account of himself. Of *course* he was the guilty party. And the same for his friend. He was just lucky to get away."

He'd swayed the men back to Sieversen. Several of them put angry gazes on the cowhand who'd spoken up.

"Thank you, Phil," Sieversen said to the merchant. "I appreciate you restoring common sense to this group."

"What're we gonna do about that Conners gal?" said the insurance salesman.

"We've already done it," Sieversen said. "Mr. Donnelly and I told her that we want her on the train this evening. And that we don't want any arguments about it."

"What'd she say?"

"Well, she tried to act like she hadn't made her mind up yet about leaving. But personally, I think she was just trying to look tough. She knows we're nobody to play around with. And while I was at it, I gave Pops Boynton holy hell for talking to her in the first place."

The blacksmith said, "Pops Boynton told my cousin he thinks we hanged the wrong man."

"Well, he won't be saying that to anybody else, believe me."

The men were getting comfortable in their defiance once again. No damned woman was going to push them around. No damned investigator from the state attorney's office was going to get any more information than he had the first time. And if Ben Tully and Pops Boynton didn't want to go along, they could damned well be put on a train and shunted off elsewhere just like the Conners gal herself.

The stage driver said, "You really think we're safe, Mr. Sieversen?"

Sieversen offered a rare and reassuring smile. He was, or so he would tell you, a natural leader of men, and one thing all natural leaders of men understood was that troops needed to be imbued with optimism and faith and hope.

"I guarantee we're safe, men," said leader of men Karl Sieversen, formerly of the United States Army. "I guarantee it."

Late in the afternoon, Tully went looking for Nan Conners. He wanted to invite her to dinner at the café. He needed to be in the company of a woman, and she was a promising one.

On the way over, he saw Susan and Delia Byrnes loading their buckboard with items they were carrying from the general store.

"When you coming out for supper, Ben?" Susan said.

"Soon as some things get cleared up, I guess."

"I heard about the girl, Nan. Mack told me about her. Said she's very pretty and very smart."

"I guess I didn't notice," Tully said. And then smiled. "Well, maybe I noticed a little bit."

Delia said, "I got some furniture polish for that table of yours. It'll look good and smell real nice, too."

"Thanks. You're sure a good girl, Delia. And a pretty one."

It was fun to make her blush. She was so shy.

•   •   •

Nan wasn't in her hotel. She wasn't anywhere to be found on the street. He stopped by Pop Boynton's, and Boynton told him about Donnelly and Sieversen telling her that she'd damned well better be on the six-oh-three.

"When was this, Pops?"

"Couple of hours ago."

"You haven't seen her since?"

"Nope. Though I'll tell you where you might look."

"Where?"

"The Catholic church. Old Gallagher said he seen her just sittin' in a pew there this mornin'. Good place to hide out if Donnelly and Sieversen were looking for you."

Tully always claimed to be a Catholic, but he wasn't much of one. Hadn't been to Mass or confession in years, hadn't in fact been in the church but once, to bury Kate.

He stood in the back of the place now, appreciating the faint odor of incense and the scent of the votive candles whose yellow-blue-red glow played off a tall statue of the Virgin. He liked Catholic ritual—he knew that when he died, he would be calling out to the Almighty for redemption—but he didn't care much for Catholic rules.

She sat in the middle of the pew about halfway up to the altar, her jaunty little hat somehow childish and dear in this sacred setting. By the angle of her tilted head, he imagined that she was looking up at the wooden cross supporting a raw, carved rendering of Christ dying. The sculpture was crude but powerful, especially as the shifting shadows of dusk—in winter, night came early now—cloaked parts of the altar, sending the sculpture into relief.

He walked up the aisle. Genuflected when he reached her pew. She didn't seem to see him. She had a rosary in her fingers. Her small mouth worked avidly at silent prayer.

He walked deep into the pew. Sat down next to her.

He didn't try to talk to her until she finished her rosary, this signified by her making the sign of the cross and touching the cross on her rosary to her lips.

He said, in barely a whisper, "I hear they want to put you on a train."

She looked at him. Her eyes weren't as clear as usual. They were shifting shadows of conflicting emotions. She nodded.

"You getting on the train?"

"That's what I came here to find out. I was hoping the Lord could tell me."

She winced suddenly, her small hand touching her abdomen.

"You all right?"

A sad little smile. "My monthly curse. For some women, it's not all that much trouble. I'm not that lucky."

"Neither was Kate. Or my mother or my sisters."

"I knew you had sisters."

"How'd you know that?"

"The way you treat women. You seem to have a sneaking suspicion that we're human beings, after all."

He laughed, his noise loud and echoing off the nave of the church. "The Lord give you His answer yet?"

"Not yet."

"You want my answer?"

"Sure. I'd appreciate it, in fact." The wince again.

"I think you should stay, and I think we should find out who killed my wife."

"You don't think it was my brother?"

"I think it could've been your brother. But I'm beginning to have serious doubts."

She reached over and gently placed the tips of her fingers on the top of his right hand. "That's a start, anyway."

"You hungry?"

"Starved."

"Me, too. Why don't I buy you some dinner at the café?"

"What happens if I'm not on that train at six-oh-three?"

"They can't run you out of town. Nobody can, unless you break the law in some way. And as far as I know, you haven't beaten up anybody or ransacked a bar. Or have you?"

"I burned down a couple of orphanages."

"Well, that's a funny thing."

"What is?"

"Pine City's got laws about anything you care to name except burning down orphanages. You can burn down as many as you like, and nobody cares. In fact, the mayor'll probably give you a plaque for it someday."

"This sounds like my kind of town." This time, her hand covered his completely. "I appreciate this, Marshal Tully."

"Ben."

"Ben."

He gave her hand a soft squeeze. "One thing you have to remember."

"I know what you're going to say."

"It's always a possibility."

"He didn't kill her. I'm sure of that."

He stood up and led them out of the pew.

Back in the vestibule, at the holy water font, she dipped her fingers in and crossed herself. He decided what the hell, he might as well, too. The water was cold on his fingertips and cold when it touched his forehead.

"You really a Catholic, Ben?"

"More than not, I guess. Why?"

"You looked sort of spooked being in here."

He smiled. "I just keep thinking about the confession I'll have to make if I ever come back to the church. They'll need three priests working around the clock."

She slid her arm through his as they reached the outside steps. "I find that hard to believe. About having all those terrible sins to confess."

"Oh, I've had my days," he said.

Swiss steak was on the menu again tonight, so they both went for that.

The café atmosphere was friendly. A number of families with tots. A number of young couples sparking. A number of older couples smiling in the glow of lamplight.

She said, "So, you haven't asked me about my scar yet."

"Figured you'd tell me when you wanted to."

"You like your Swiss steak?"

"Like it fine. You?"

"It's really good. So, do you want me to tell you?"

"You're kind of working up to it, huh?"

She laughed. "Yeah. It always takes me a little while."

"Well, that's what we've got. A little while."

"What time is it, by the way?"

"Let's see now." He took his railroad watch out of his shirt pocket behind the badge. "Five-forty-seven."

"They're probably at the depot. Waiting for me."

"Probably."

She took another bite of food. "Boy, this really is good. Wish *we* had a café like this." She inhaled deeply, the way a young girl might, and then settled in to tell her story.

"My dad did it."

"The scar?"

"Umm-hmm."

"On purpose?"

"Umm-hmm."

"Why would he do something like that?"

"Said he was doing me a favor. Said he was making sure that I'd make a good, faithful wife when my time came. Said my mother wouldn't have run around with other men if she hadn't been cursed with such a pretty face."

"Did she run around on him?"

"Yeah, unfortunately. I never knew which came first, the beatings or her running around. He always said he wouldn't've beat her if she hadn't run around, and she always said she wouldn't've run around if he hadn't beat her. Francis Xavier was so big by the time he was twelve that he started stepping in. He could manhandle my dad by then. And every time my dad tried to beat my mother, Francis Xavier would stop him. He couldn't stop her from running around, though, and neither could I and neither could the parish priest. Everybody knew our business. Said we were trash, especially my mom. We always sat in the back pew in the church so people couldn't stare at us. And we'd leave a few minutes before the Mass ended so we could get in our buggy and be gone by the time everybody gathered to gossip outdoors." She shrugged with great enchanting delicacy. "So, anyway, that's how I got my scar."

"Where's your dad now?"

"Dead. So's my mom. Dad got into some bad liquor, and it made him blind and out of his mind for a couple of days—he kept screaming about devils coming to get him—and then it killed him. And about a year later, Mom got this thing in her heart—I can't remember what they called it—and keeled over one day right in front of Francis Xavier and me, and died right in the kitchen. Our dog Rusty kept licking her forehead, like he was trying to bring her back or something. I remember that it was so sad and funny at the same time—you know how things can be like that sometimes—Rusty just licking and licking her forehead, and when we swatted him away, he'd come right back and lick her forehead some more."

Tully only half-heard the last couple of her sentences because by now he'd spotted them in the doorway. Donnelly and Sieversen. Their scowls said there was going to be trouble.

Ben and Nan were sitting at a small table near the back, where the room became an L leading back to the kitchen. Donnelly and Sieversen hadn't spotted them yet, but they were about to.

By now, Nan had seen them.

"My escorts."

"Looks that way."

Donnelly and Sieversen saw them. Started back. Their air was so severe, people started watching them, knowing instinctively that something was about to happen. Even before he'd drawn within speaking range, Sieversen said, "I thought we had an agreement, young lady."

"I didn't agree to anything, Mr. Sieversen." She looked at Tully.

"Why don't you men sit down and have some coffee?" Tully said.

"You know damned well there's no *time* for coffee," Sieversen said. "She needs to get over to the depot and get her ticket."

"She doesn't need a ticket."

"Why not?" Sieversen said.

"Because she's not going anyplace."

"You don't have anything to do with this, Tully," Sieversen said. "I've been talking to the mayor. You may not even have a job much longer, so I'd advise that you just keep your mouth shut."

Donnelly once again restrained his impetuous friend. "Why don't we have a cup of coffee, like the marshal here says?"

"There isn't time."

"There's a little time. So let's just sit down and cool off a little."

Donnelly the diplomat. Donnelly the benefactor. Because of it, people had a hard time hating him, even though they knew how he sometimes undermined the town. Even respectable people liked Donnelly.

They ordered their coffees. While they waited, they sat and stared at each other. Uncomfortably. One or two of them would look as if they were about to say something, but somehow the words never materialized. Tully watched the various customers. Nan looked for something in her bag. Donnelly went through the elaborate ritual of preparing his stogie for smoking. Good old Sieversen just sat there and scowled with baronial displeasure.

Finally, their coffee. Finally, they started talking again.

Sieversen said, "We had an agreement."

"No, we didn't, Mr. Sieversen."

"People around here call me the Colonel."

"All right, then . . . Colonel. We didn't have an agreement. I was just trying to be polite. I wanted to think over what you'd said. And I have thought it over. And I've decided to stay.

"He put you up to this, didn't he?" Sieversen snapped. "The marshal here."

"He didn't put me up to anything. I have a mind of my own, believe it or not. And I've decided to stay." In a lower voice, one reflecting her pain, she said, "The man you hung was my brother, and I loved him, very much, and I believe he was innocent, and I plan to stay here and prove it."

"Not if we don't let you, you won't stay here."

"And just how will you stop me, Colonel? I haven't broken any laws. I have money. I have a good reputation. There's no legal way you can make me leave."

Sieversen glared at Tully. "The town did this man a favor, which he's too unappreciative to accept. We spared him the pain of dragging this whole thing out. I might say we did the same for you, Miss Conners. The pain of seeing your brother in court. The pain of waiting for execution day. Do you really believe he wouldn't have been found guilty in this county, Miss Conners? When he was found with blood on his hands and things from Kate Tully's house in his pocket?"

The force of his words—many onlookers gaping now—silenced her for a moment. Then, quietly, she said, "I'm not going, Colonel. I want to stay here a few more days."

Donnelly spoke for the first time. "This isn't going to help anybody, Miss Conners. It's just going to stir things up again. The lynching wasn't the right way to handle this; I can see that now. I told you that this afternoon. But the Colonel's right. A jury would certainly have found your brother guilty. I'm sorry to say that for your sake. But I'm afraid it's true." He looked up at clock on the wall. "There's still time to catch that train, Miss Conners. And we've even got you a nice little parting gift. We'd planned to give it to you at the depot, but we may as well give it to you here."

From the pocket inside his suit coat, he took a white business envelope and handed it over to her. "Take a look inside."

She did so.

Tully could see what it was. But he couldn't see how much it was.

"There's a thousand dollars in there, Miss Conners," Donnelly said in a particularly paternal tone of voice. "This should help you start a new life for yourself back home. We just want you to know that the people of Pine City wish you well."

He was smiling right up to the moment when she pushed the envelope across the table, back to him.

"I can't take your money, Mr. Donnelly, though I appreciate the offer."

"So you thought you could handle her, huh?" said Colonel Sieversen, formerly of the United States Army.

Tully said, "You've had your say. Now we'd like to finish our meals."

"There's still time to get that train," Donnelly said, standing up.

"If she changes her mind, I'll see that she gets there on time.

"Good evening, everybody," Donnelly said with an attempt at gallantry.

"There are going to be a lot of people unhappy about this, let me tell you that," Sieversen said. "A lot of them."

"Come on, Colonel," Donnelly said. "Let's let these folks finish their meal in peace."

They turned to face a café full of people intrigued by what had been going on at that table in the back. This would be good for a week's worth of gossip, the story told and told until it bore no resemblance at all to what had actually happened. What good was a story about four people sitting at a table talking? Maybe the marshal started to make a play for his gun. Maybe the Colonel slapped the marshal with his glove, daring him to an old-fashioned duel. Maybe the lass used an exquisitely filthy word in rebuffing the Colonel. That was the nice thing about real events. They could be gussied up and fussed up in so many different ways.

"You were good," Tully said.

She smiled. "I wasn't bad, was I?"

They didn't leave the café until after eight o clock. By this time, the temperature had dropped several degrees, and people were hurrying home to fireplaces and stoves and warm beds. Frost gleamed in the moonlight along the boardwalk as they strolled back to her hotel.

"I still think you should follow up on Rafe Simmons."

"I guess it wouldn't hurt to take a ride out there tomorrow. See what he was doing the night Kate was killed."

"I'll go with you, if you'd like me to."

He laughed. "I'm not sure the citizens would appreciate me bringing you along. That could cause some trouble."

"I'm kind've pushing you hard, aren't I?"

"Maybe a little bit."

"You just tell me to back off whenever you want to."

"Oh, you'll know when I want you to back off, believe me."

They were passing down the block that belonged to Donnelly's various enterprises, including his two saloons and his casino. Happy sounds emerged—of the player piano, live fiddles, drunks of various types, the slap of cards being put down, the grind of the roulette wheel, croupier calls to place your bets.

The streets were shadowy. The tall lamps created small pools of light, but there were wide areas of deep shadows between them.

In the noise and the darkness, Tully slipped into his own thoughts, mostly about Nan's father's decision to inflict that hellacious scar on his daughter. Must've been quite a man, that one.

He saw her start to collapse even before the sound of the bullet had quite registered on his hearing. She was crumpling in half, already starting to lean forward, her sweet little hat falling from her head as she pitched toward the boardwalk. He wasn't even sure where she'd been shot.

He reacted quickly, sliding his arm around her waist and bringing her down to the boardwalk right along with him. Another bullet ripped into a hitching post; and then another tore into the boardwalk about a foot ahead of where their heads lay.

By now, Tully had his .45 out and was firing blindly at the

dark alley across the street. The shooter had the advantage. He was using a carbine.

But the bullets drove the shooter away. A shape shifted in the alley shadows; moonlight gleamed momentarily on the long, silver barrel of a carbine. And then the shape was running, running hard toward the far end of the alley.

Tully turned to Nan now, and what he saw appalled him. The bullet had entered near the top of her skull at the back of her head.

The shots had brought out a crowd.

Batwing doors were flung wide as some of the many denizens of Donnelly's saloons and casino came down the steps to see what had happened.

Tully paid no attention.

He had only one thing on his mind.

Finding a pulse in neck, wrist, or ankle.

Maybe it was the way he was doing it. Maybe his panic and rage made him incompetent.

But whatever the cause, he couldn't find even the faintest of pulses anywhere on Nan. Not even the faintest.

# PART THREE

# ONE

A S MUCH AS Ralph Donnelly had loved his wife Ruth,
he had never had much time for her family. They were
river rats who'd grown up along the Mississippi near New
Orleans. What had saved her from their fate—the few times
he'd met them they'd been so unwashed and so uncouth and
so uneducated that they resembled a subspecies of the
human race—was that they had virtually sold her into slav-
ery when she was eight years old, traded her for a fishing
shanty owned by a local member of the gentry, a woman
who was losing her sight and wanted a white girl to become
her eyes in the coming years. The woman, educated, kind,
caring, had lost both her husband and son in the previous
year and so, except for her even dozen housecats, had no one
on whom to visit her love. The girl became very much like
a daughter, staying with the old woman until not only the old
woman's eyes but heart as well gave out. Donnelly met Ruth
a year later. This was in that time when gambling boats only
enhanced the romance of the big river. He was a fair poker
player, even better when he cheated, which was most of the
time. He fell purely and sorely in love with the woman because she'd been the first woman he'd ever felt respect for.

And protective of. His mother had been a harsh streetwalker in Baltimore. She'd never made the slightest attempt to care for him. But this young woman—no beauty, but then Donnelly wasn't exactly a beauty, either—loved him with equal passion and respect. She would give him a home, a family, and respectability, three things he had longed for.

She'd never heard much from her river rat family until they somehow learned that her husband was a man of substantial means. And then the letters began pouring in.

They obviously had to have somebody else write the letters for them. They were lucky they could sign X on contracts.

The letters were all tales of woe. This child was sick; that child couldn't go to school because there wasn't enough money; a roof had caved in; the old horse finally gave out and died. And on and on.

It was probably cruel—and every once in a while, the two of them laughed about it—but the Donnellys spent many an hour going over the letters and sneering. Never had God visited so much suffering—allegedly, anyway—upon such a small group of people. Job and Moses didn't know what suffering was compared to these folks.

Just in case a few of these fanciful pleas were based in fact—their favorite down the years was the Indian raid (and just what Indians were they referring to, exactly?) in which "Pa" got two arrows in his chest and one in his head but somehow managed to recover, being apparently of superhuman breeding stock—they sent checks every once in a while. Once in awhile—probably to assuage their guilt over laughing at so many of the letters—they'd send substantial sums, just assuming it would all be spent on liquor, gambling, and Lord only knew what other vices the river rats had developed over the years.

The letters had ceased following Ruth's death. But now the river rats had started writing again. And always said the same thing at the beginning: "We know that Ruth would want you to know, Uncle Ralph (every one of the river rats, be they adult or child, called him Uncle Ralph), that things aren't all they could be for our family these days. Followed immediately by the latest tragedy in the most dramatic of terms. Donnelly's favorite was still: "If you could have seen Pug's eye hanging out of its socket—well, to make that eye right again, Pug's going to need an operation, and right fast, too." Pug, one of the most repellent of God's creatures, had already lost one ear, part of his nose, all of his teeth, three fingers, two toes, and had an "alligator-like patch of skin" on his left cheek from falling face first into a campfire. Couldn't they spread all these misfortunes around a little bit? Why pick on Pug all the time? He should be dead by now. Although, when you thought about it, coming from the same stock that produced a man who could survive two arrows in the chest and one in the head, Pug was probably a pretty resilient lad.

The latest installment of the river rat saga had to do with "six black-and-white milk cows that just up and vanished. We expect rustlers."

*"Suspect,"* Donnelly said to himself. "Not *expect.*" Not even the person writing these letters was smart.

But then he realized that he should be grateful for this letter. It kept him from thinking about and killing the Conners woman.

With that young gal in town now—Nan Conners—things didn't seem as certain as they once did. If she started prying into things—

The front door opened and thundered shut. Donnelly set his pen down, stood up, and went to the study door.

He went to the landing and looked down into the vestibule just in time to see Frank crumple to the floor blacked out, as usual, by demon rum.

If that Conners gal ever started asking real serious questions . . .

There was a lot of solemn doctor talk. Doc Daly's nurse, a warhorse named Reva, was called from a warm bed to assist. This had come at a good time, early enough that Doc was still reasonably sober. His hands hadn't started to shake yet, always a good sign when a critical operation was at hand. The most reassuring thing of all was that Daly was skilled at extracting bullets from just about any part of the body you cared to name. He'd started out as an animal doctor—well, he'd actually started out as an animal doctor's assistant but had worked up from there—and then took what he knew about animals and applied it to humans. As he liked to say, "I don't have no fancy diploma. I just have the common sense the good Lord give me." His office was always cluttered with new medical journals. Tully couldn't figure out if they were just window dressing or if the man actually read them.

Tully was not patient enough to sit in the outer office. He decided to go back to the alley where the shooter had been. He'd roused a couple of auxiliary deputies and told them to guard both entrances to the alley. He didn't want people tramping around in there. He was big on journals, same as Doc Daly. His law enforcement journals said that a good deal of evidence could be found where the criminal had stood. Comb and sift through everything carefully, his journals urged. He'd need light of day to do a complete job. But now he had a lantern hooked in his hand and wanted to do a little preliminary work.

Nobody was bothering the auxiliary deputies. Everybody'd gone back to the saloons. It was more fun being in where it was nice and warm—and where you could keep telling the barkeep you wanted another one—than standing out in the dark somewhere freezing your ass off.

The first half hour—always worrying when Doc Daly would send a runner to tell him that the operation was over and that he could come in and see young Nan Conners—he didn't find much at all. All the usual: scraps of paper, busted glass, animal droppings. Then, out the service entrance to the café, he saw where somebody had thrown out a pail of water. The sandy soil of the alley was a ragged, damp circle a few feet from the door. The soft lantern light didn't pick up the boot prints at first. But when he brought the lantern

closer to the wet spot, he saw the indentations the boots had
made.

He wasn't sure what to make of the prints. They might
well mean nothing. The shape of the heel and sole were
common. So was the size, maybe a nine or ten wide. He
leaned even closer to the imprints and it was then he saw it.
Something resembling an *N* in the center of the heel.

Recognition didn't come instantly. It played at the edge of
his awareness for a time. The *N* signified something familiar, but what? And in the end, somebody else had to figure it
out for him.

He called over one of the auxiliary deputies, a skinny man
named Widdams who spent his days as a bookkeeper in a
lumberyard. Widdams had an Adam's apple so pronounced,
it looked as if it was going to rip through his neck. It was almost painful to watch him swallow.

"Freezing my nuts off, Marshal. You think I could get
some coffee? Hogan's freezing *his* nuts, too."

"I'll have somebody bring you both some coffee."

"Appreciate it. I'm real susceptible to catching cold. My
mom said she never seen nobody who caught as many colds
as I do."

Tully almost smiled. Auxiliary deputies were little boys in
grown-up bodies who had always wanted to be lawmen.
Well, a certain type of lawman, the type of lawman who
strode the streets on sunny days winning the secret passion
of the ladies and the obvious respect of men, the type of lawmen who put dime-novel heroes to shame: resolutely honest,
brave, relentless.

But most of them were like Widdams here. The few times
local law enforcement saw fit to use them was usually when
a disaster had taken place: a bad fire, a flood, a blizzard. And
they were always in charge of keeping people away or moving people along or seeing that people didn't get in the way
of doctors or nurses or real lawmen going about their duties.

Not real exciting or romantic work, no women swooning
at the sight of them, no men showing granite-eyed respect.

Indeed, most townspeople sort of sniggered at them, amused that grown men would still cherish such childhood fantasies.

"Look at this here," Tully said

"Where?"

"Lean closer."

"It's an imprint of a boot."

"That's right. Now look *real* close."

"It's a letter."

"Yes. It's an *N*. But what does it stand for?"

"Well, hell, Marshal," Widdams said, straightening up. "It stands for Needham. The cobbler."

"Damn," Tully said.

"What?"

"I should've thought of that. Needham is right. But I didn't know he put an *N* on heels."

"Oh, yeah. On his tailor-mades."

"He hand sews boots?"

"If you've got the money and the time.

Tully was grateful for all the help Widdams had been. "You know what, Widdams? I'm not only going to send you over some coffee. I'm going to have the café send you over some pastries, too."

Widdams grinned like a birthday boy. "You be sure and tell that to Hogan, too. He's freezing his nuts even more than I am."

The temperature was in the high forties.

"I'll be happy to tell him."

As soon as he started walking away from the alley—after giving Hogan the good news about the coffee and the pastries—Tully fell into gloom again.

He wondered if Nan Conners was going to live out the night.

Mary Kay Washburn knew it was dangerous. But that was what made it sort of appealing.

She waited until the other men had gone to bed—they were early and heavy sleepers—and then she went up the stairs to Mr. Langley's room.

The earlier excitement of the evening was over now, the shooting down in the business district. The young woman whose brother had been hanged.

Mary Kay Washburn had no interest in it. Mr. Langley was her one and only interest. When he'd first come here and she'd gone through his room—the prerogative of all landladies, as she saw it—he'd had a few clothes and not much else.

Funny he should mention, as he had earlier, coming into money, because he'd bought himself some good clothes while in town here, including a pair of expensive new boots that he had Needham the cobbler make up special for him.

She eased up the stairs. Every single one of them made so darned much noise in the quiet of the hushed house. Only the ticking of the grandfather clock made any sound outside of them.

At the top of the stairs, she was greeted with a ragged symphony of snoring, coughing, dream-muttering, and nightmare-gasping. The typical noises workingmen made while sleeping.

Mr. Langley's place was near the end of the hall. She went there immediately. Put her ear to the door. He might have snuck up the back way. Some of the men did sometimes, especially if they'd been drinking heavily. Mary Kay Washburn did not approve of excessive drinking and was not afraid to say so, whether they were sober enough to remember her admonitions or not.

Silence on the other side of Mr. Langley's door.

She pushed the door open with great care and caution.

The room smelled of cigarette tobacco, whiskey, male cologne, sleep, sweat, jism. She remembered that last scent from the days when she and the mister had made love frequently. She thought of him so heavy on top of her, grunting, funny and oddly dear at the same time. He never could satisfy her but she always pretended he could. A strange thought, one she'd never had before: Had she satisfied *him?* She knew he stayed an awfully long time in the bathroom sometimes. And once in his bureau she'd found a French postcard, a rather bovine nude woman, with her legs spread wide, a great vulgar distance wide, bearishly hairy down there and no bosom to speak of at all. Had he gotten more satisfaction from a postcard than he had from her? She'd felt terrible and knew she would worry this, the way she worried most things, for years to come. She'd never confronted him about the postcard. But perhaps she should have. And perhaps she should've taken him in her mouth the way he'd always wanted her to. Oh, Lord—and she knew this to be true—she'd worry this not just for weeks but months. Months and months and months.

As a way of distracting herself, she went about searching Langley's room.

The expected, that was all she found. A number of new shirts, collars, jackets. He'd be wearing the new boots. A stack of what appeared to be theatrical reviews.

"Langley a Sensation in The Rancher's Daughter!"

"Langley Triumphs Again—Road Show Better Than NYC Original!"

"Langley Shows How It Should Be Done!"

There were probably twenty such reviews. Not until she looked at them more carefully—carrying them over into the moonlight coming through the window did she notice that they all bore the same typeface. These weren't taken from different newspapers. They were all of a piece. She strongly suspected that Langley had written them himself and then had them printed up by some cheap print house somewhere.

"Langley triumphs again," she smirked to herself.

She went back to work.

Under the only chair, she found another stack of theatrical reviews. Under the bed, she found a stash of dirty postcards not unlike the one her husband had owned. There seemed to be a premium on girls with hairy crotches. Under the bureau, she found—

And that's when she heard it.

A faint squeak, the sigh of old wood under the pressure of something heavy. A human body, say.

And then the door was open, and there stood Mr. Langley in all his arrogant glory.

He had his Colt drawn. Silhouetted this way—faint lamplight behind him—he looked larger and more threatening than he ever had. His wide-brimmed hat was especially dramatic.

Her position made her even more vulnerable, bent down this way to pull the kind of bag a bank uses to carry money out from under the bureau.

But the name stenciled on it wasn't that of a bank but rather Carter's Jewelers.

"If I hadn't spent time with a lady already this evening, I might've joined you down there on the floor, Mrs. Washburn."

She got up, brushing her hands off on her faded housedress. "If you lay a hand on me, I'll scream."

" 'I'm the one who should be screaming, Mrs. Washburn. I come home to find that my room—the very room that I paid a good bit of money for—has been invaded by a burglar."

"Burglar, pah," she said, turning up the lamp.

"Well, what would you call somebody who enters somebody else's private room without permission?"

"You know I'm no burglar."

She hated his coyness, his teasing, his arrogance.

"Then what were you doing? Were you cleaning at this hour, Mrs. Washburn? I'm the first to appreciate a good cleaning, Mrs. Washburn. But not at this hour, and not without knowing in advance that you're going to be here,"

"I'm going now," she said and started to push past him,

But he grabbed her, hard, by the wrist.

"So did you find anything interesting?"

"Let go of me."

"What were you looking for, Mrs. Washburn?"

"Nothing. I just wanted to make sure you hadn't skipped out."

"And what if I had? You know that my rent is paid up, Mrs. Washburn."

"I—"

He slammed her elbow with the palm of his hand. This only enhanced the pain in her wrist. Tears glistened in her eyes.

"What did you find?"

"Nothing.

"I want the truth."

The coyness was gone from his voice. She saw him looking around the room. She wondered if he'd seen her looking beneath the bureau. Given the position of bed and bureau, he might have thought she was looking under the bed.

God, she hoped he didn't know what she'd found under the bureau.

So that's why he was in town. He'd robbed the stage a few weeks ago, taking all of Mr. Carter's money and diamonds and gems.

"I didn't find anything. Honest."

He gave her wrist a final sharp wrench, then let her go.

"A man of a more suspicious nature might not let you go so easily."

She rubbed her wrist. The pain shot all the way into her shoulder now.

"If I find anything missing, I'm coming downstairs for you.

Her face was tense, angry. "You said you were leaving tomorrow. I want you out of here by nine A.M."

"You don't have to worry about that, Mrs. Washburn. I'll be glad to get out of here. I'm tired of watching you flounce around with those cow teats of yours bouncing up and down all the time. Has anybody ever told you, Mrs. Washburn, that as a seductress you're pathetic? Your boarders laugh about you. Really. They all have their little favorite jokes about how you sashay around pretending to be some femme fatale when you're nothing more than an old cow. Don't you ever look in the mirror, Mrs. Washburn? Don't you ever see yourself as you really are? You're probably afraid to. And if I was you, I'm sure I'd be afraid to, too. You're a joke, Mrs. Washburn, a sick, sad old joke. Now, will you kindly remove your fat, unpleasant self from my room so I can get some sleep?"

He couldn't hurt her with gun or knife. But he could certainly hurt her with words.

She stood there stunned, unable to move, think.

Nobody had ever said things this hateful to her.

And the worst thing was that she recognized truth in his words.

All her fantasies about all her boarders desiring her.

Well, she'd never again be able to walk around the house imagining that they wanted her. Instead, she'd see their once-secret smirks as she started to leave the room, hear their once-secret jokes as she walked in on them at dinner-time.

Laughing at her.

*"Your cow teats bouncing up and down."*

Isn't that what he'd said? And even worse, wasn't that the truth? The truth some part of her had always known? The truth she'd never been able to face?

She thought of the mister's French postcard.

Even the mister hadn't been able to stand her.

She put her hands over her face and ran sobbing down the stairs.

# TWO

AROUND TWO A.M., Doc Daly came out of his operating room and said, "You're gonna ask me how she's doing, Tully, and I'm going to tell you I don't have no idea at all."

"You got the bullet out?"

Daly was drying his hands after scrubbing up real good. You could hear his nurse back there cleaning things up.

Tully had been smoking cigarettes and drinking coffee to stay awake. Huge emotions—fear, hope, rage—warred within him. His mind buzzed from the effects of the nicotine and the caffeine.

Daly said, "Nothing to get out. The bullet passed out of her head clean. And it hadn't been in deep. It's gauging the effects of it. Doesn't look like there was a lot of damage, since it wasn't much deeper than a flesh wound would be. But we're dealing with the brain here. I'm not going to bullshit you, Tully. This is way beyond what I normally do."

"Is she conscious?"

Daly shrugged. "Not so's you'd notice. She's muttering to herself. Can't make any of it out. She kind of goes in and

out, and that's what scares me. I did everything I know how
to do. I just hope it was enough."

"Can I see her?"

"Sure."

He went into the operating room. He wasn't squeamish,
but he wasn't eager to see a lot of blood, either, especially
when it came from somebody he cared about.

Reva Mulverne, the nurse, said, "She's a pretty little
thing." Then she smiled. "But I bet you already noticed that,
didn't you, Marshal?"

He smiled. "Yeah, I guess I did notice that a couple of
times, now that you mention it." The smile felt good, hope-
ful.

Reva was scrubbing everything down with soap and
water and some kind of disinfectant powder. The combined
odors were harsh.

The room doubled as an examination room: glass-fronted
cabinets with a variety of medicines and surgical instru-
ments, with the padded operating table that could be folded
up and used as a chair. Bloody towels and rags were everywhere.

Her face was wan, almost deathlike. He thought of how
hard her period was and felt sorry for her. This trip wasn't
working out for her. No hard proof that her brother was innocent, hard cramps from her period, and now being shot in
the head.

"She asked for you a couple of times, Marshal."

For some reason, that made him feel better.

"The two of you must've gotten to be pretty good friends,
huh?"

"You going to start some stories about us, Reva?"

Reva had the grace to smile. "You know me, Marshal.
Tight-lipped."

He laughed. "Sure you are, Reva."

Reva was a better form of getting the news out than the
newspaper could ever be. A small-town doctor knows all the
secrets, and so does his nurse. Reva, a hardy fifty-year-old
with strawlike gray hair and a pair of hands that would do a

champion boxer nicely, told stories not in a malicious way especially but just because she liked to talk. God forbid you had a serious medical ailment you wanted to keep secret. By the time you got home from the doctor's office, Reva would have it all over town.

Nan stirred momentarily. Eyelids fluttered. Mouth opened. A deep, little-girl-sleep sigh.

He touched her damp forehead, surprised to find that it was neither hot nor cold but just about right.

"You find out who did it?"

"Nope."

"Lot of people didn't want her here."

"So I'm told."

"Maybe it'd be better if everybody just kinda forgot what happened and went on with their lives, Marshal."

He glanced up. "You're throwing in with Donnelly and that crowd, huh?"

"Not throwing in exactly," she said, wiping sweat from her forehead with the back of her hand. "Just seeing the wisdom in letting it go to ground. Forgetting about it. She seems like a nice little gal, and I'm real sorry somebody shot her. But just because she's a nice gal don't mean that her brother was innocent." She listed all the facts that everybody always did when concluding that Francis Xavier Conners was the killer. "Seems like that sure makes him guilty."

"Maybe."

The door opened. Daly was back. "You sure you want to stay here all night with her, Reva?"

"You need your sleep worse'n I do. You got patients all day long tomorrow.

"Clete won't like it."

She laughed. "I'll put socks on his feet. The only reason he'll miss me is because I won't be there to keep his feet warm."

"Well," Daly said, "I appreciate it."

"I think I'll be staying, too."

They both looked surprised at Tully's words.

"Whoever tried to kill her might come back to get her."

"You know," Reva said, "I never thought of that."

"We can sleep in shifts," Tully said. "There's still five hours before dawn. We can grab a couple of hours of sleep, anyway."

"That's the advantage of being young," Daly said to Reva. "You spring chickens can stay up all night and still function in the morning. Whereas old fogies like me need our sleep."

He slapped his derby on his head, tucked a half-smoked stogie in the corner of his mouth and, with his Gladstone bag in tow, left his office.

The train was twenty-one hours late—not exactly unheard of in this area and pulled into the depot about the time Daly was leaving the office.

Jim Van Amburg, the deputy who'd handcuffed Lawson to his right wrist, stood on the depot platform, now partaking deeply of the clean, chill night air.

"I have to piss," Lawson said.

"You have to piss more'n any prisoner I ever transported."

"That's 'cause so many deppities like you pounded on my kidneys so long."

"I shoulda figgered it was the law's fault. You blame us for everything else."

"I hate law."

"No kiddin'? I never woulda guessed it."

"And yer about the dumbest shit lawman I ever been with."

Van Amburg shook his head. "You ain't much to travel with, either, I'll sure tell you that. Lots of men, we try 'n' get to know each other."

"Buddies, huh?"

"Something like that. And I know you're bein' sarcastic. But friendly like, anyway. You got to be together a long time and handcuffed together like we are, might as well get to know each other a little bit and all, and talk about your kinfolk and what you'd like to do someday and things like that. But all you done the whole trip was bitch, and I got to tell you, I'm mighty sick of it. I've never been so glad to get rid of a prisoner in my life."

"Gee, I'm sorry to hear that."

Van Amburg, all smells and rashes and belches and dirty clothes, all eye matter and nose booger and oily farts, a mean prick on the one hand but sort of a sad bumpkin on the other, Van Amburg, thoroughly sick of him now, grabbed Lawson by the arm and said, "Let's go find the marshal's office so I can dump you off and get you the hell out of my life."

"Can't be soon enough for me."

"They might lynch you here, Lawson, same as they did your partner. You ever think of that?"

"You tryin' to scare me?"

"Sure. You gonna tell me that ain't crossed your mind?"

"It's crossed my mind."

"I'm just sorry I won't be here to see it is all," Deppity Van Amburg said.

Then he gave his prisoner's arm a good hard jerk and dragged him along to the marshal's office.

Mack Byrnes, first thing he saw Tully next morning, rushed up and said, "We have a visitor in back."

"Oh? Probably the governor."

Byrnes laughed. "Well, close. Lawson. Conners's friend."

"What the hell time did he get in?"

"Around three, I guess. Kepler was here."

"You talk to him?"

"A little bit. He isn't real friendly. And I guess I don't blame him. He thinks we're trying to hang Kate's murder on him."

"Anything else I should know about?" Tully asked, settling in behind his desk with a steaming cup of coffee.

"I was going to ask you that. How's Nan Conners doing?"

"Too early to tell, according to Reva Mulverne."

"Well, she should know. She's a lot smarter than the doc is."

That was the conventional wisdom in town here. That

without Reva, Daly wouldn't be able to so much as put io-
dine on a tiny cut.

"Well, I didn't get it straight from Reva herself—she's
home sleeping-but according to the doc, Nan Conners is
holding her own.

He started through his mail. He was just groggy enough
to have overlooked the note Byrnes had left on the corner of
his desk.

Tully picked it up.

"Figured you'd see that eventually."

"Aw, shit, this sure isn't what I need this morning."

"The way I get it, they're holding you responsible for her
being shot."

"As opposed to the sonofabitch who actually shot her,
you mean?"

"You know how they think, Marshal. If Ben Tully had put
her right on a train soon as she got here, none of this
would've happened. So it's really Ben Tully's fault."

"That's how they think, all right."

"So the mayor wants to see you in his office at ten."

"And if I don't show up?"

"He told me to tell you that if you don't show up, he'll
come looking for you."

"Yeah, him or Donnelly or Sieversen."

"You think they had anything to do with the shooting?"

"You mean you *don't* think they did, Mack?"

"I got to admit it's at least a possibility." Tully picked up
his cup of coffee. Inhaled some of the steam. Closed his eyes
to enjoy it even more. He said, "I need to stop over at the
cobbler's. Then I'll go see the mayor."

"Better than him having to come over here looking for
you. Oh, and Susan and I were thinking maybe you'd like to
stop out for dinner tonight."

"I appreciate it, Mack. But let's see how the day goes
first. I may just go home and collapse after work."

"Any special time you going to see Lawson?"

"Soon as I get back from the mayor's, I suppose."

"He wants a lawyer."

Tully shrugged. "Hell, get him one. Get him O'Shea. He's always bitching about how bad the poor prisoners have it. O'Shea and this Lawson sound like they'll get along real fine."

Harvey Needham's cobbler shop had a tiny, merry bell just above the door so Harvey could hear you in case he was in back. The air was rich with the smells of dozens of dyes and polishes and leather tanners.

Harvey was stoop-shouldered from bending over his work for so many years. His thick, stained fingers moved with surprising artistry as he patched, rebuilt, and stained boots and shoes piled on a table behind the small wooden counter near the front of his tiny place of business. He was short enough that he had to look up at Tully from an uncomfortable-looking angle.

"I'll have them boots for you in a couple days, Marshal."

"I'm here about boots, all right. But not mine."

"Not yours?"

Tully explained what he'd found in the alley. "So, do you make a lot of custom-fit boots.?"

"Not many, no. Kind of expensive for most folks. They buy outta the Monkey Ward catalog or Sears. Or down to Wainwright's by the river. Damned things ain't no good, but they don't have money for nothing better."

"You keep records of your work?"

"More or less. That way if somebody wants another pair, I got the measurements on file and everything."

Tully reached in his pocket. "Well, I traced over the outline I found in the alley last night. People tell me the *N* in the heel means you made it." He showed Needham the tracing he'd made.

"Yep, that's mine, all right," Needham said. "Course I'd have to measure it and look it up in my records and see whose foot it is."

"I'd appreciate you doing that as soon as possible."

"I could probably have the information for you in half an hour."

"That'd be fine. I'll stop back or have one of my deputies stop back."

Needham was in the process of saddle-soaping a dried-out lady's boot. "Don't know why they don't take care of their footwear. Last two, three times as long if they did. People just don't think things through, Marshal. You ever notice that?"

"Yeah, I've noticed that," Tully said. "More than a couple times, in fact."

# THREE

MARY KAY WASHBURN walked to the bottom of the stairs at 8:58 A.M. She had told Langley she wanted him out of here by 9:00 A.M., and she meant it. To bolster her resolve, she had her husband's old Civil War pistol. There was something wrong with it—God knew what—but Langley didn't know that.

She carried it in case he decided to get rough or something.

At 8:59 A.M., she heard his door open, his booted feet come into the hall, his door close, his booted feet proceed to the landing and begin their walk down the stairs.

"Ah, Mrs. Washburn," he said when he was at midpoint on the steps, "I see you have a gun. Are we going to have a shoot-out?"

"I just want you out of here."

"Carrying a gun, I'm afraid, distracts from the delicate nature of your beautiful face.

"Nobody ever talked to me the way you did yesterday, said hurtful, awful things like that."

He now stood on the floor, facing her. "Then I would assume you've managed to surround yourself with flatterers and liars, Mrs. Washburn. Because I wasn't speaking just for myself; I was speaking, as I said, for every man in this house."

"Get out of here."

He carried a carpetbag and a leather grip, the same two pieces he'd brought in with him.

"I don't suppose you have a photograph of yourself I could take with me, do you? I wouldn't want to forget my pleasant stay under your roof."

And then he bowed the way actors bowed, deep and stagy, and walked to the vestibule.

"I don't suppose you'd open the front door for me, would you?" He shook his head, his dramatic hat looking larger than ever. "I didn't think so."

He tucked his leather grip under his arm and opened the front door with his free hand.

"Good-bye, Mrs. Washburn." He gave her his chilliest of smirks and walked out of her life.

It was as if a clamorous parade had passed out of earshot. All the turbulent emotions he'd wakened in her—anger, humiliation, scorn, and a need for vengeance—these had filled her head with thoughts that threatened to overwhelm her, made any thought of peace of mind or sleep impossible.

He saw her as powerless. Well, she wasn't. She'd seen the canvas bag belonging to Carter's Jewelry. And she knew now damned well why he'd come to town here. He was escaping with a great deal of money.

If only she'd been able to find that jewelry in his room yesterday . . .

But there was another way for her to rob him—rob him of his arrogance and disdain. And freedom.

She would go find Marshal Tully and tell him exactly what she'd seen.

And then Tully would take care of Mr. Langley for her.

She was the only one in the house. The men were at work, She'd cleaned up the dining room and kitchen after breakfast. She really should start on the parlor now. But that would have to wait until she got back.

She kept remembering the things Mr. Langley had said to her yesterday. What if they were true? What if her boarders really did regard her as grotesque, as he had claimed? Last night, she'd been convinced that his words were true. But now she wasn't so sure.

She'd watched the men at breakfast this morning. They seemed as friendly and courtly as ever. *"Here, let me help you with those dishes, Mrs. Washburn."* And *"My, aren't we looking especially fine, this morning, Mrs. Washburn?"* *"Say, I heard you playing the piano and singing in the parlor last night, Mrs. Washburn, and you've sure got a beautiful voice. I just hope some handsome dog don't come along and steal you from us, Mrs. Washburn. Then where would we be?"*

Did any of *that* sound like men who were repelled by her, secretly or otherwise?

Hardly.

She went to get her wrap.

*I'll tell Marshal Tully about the canvas bag, and we'll see where Mr. Smart-Mouth is then, thrown in jail with a bunch of drunkards and coloreds and sodomites and God alone knows what else. I'll bet Mr. Smart-Mouth doesn't insult any of them. All those stories the men on my porch tell about tales they've heard of prison life. We'll see how he does behind bars after all those terrible men get done with him.*

Then she was in the street. Walking fast. Looking for Tully.

Bert Lawson said, "I didn't have no advantages in life, that's my problem. If I'd've had advantages, I'd sure as hell have turned out better."

"A lot of men who didn't have advantages turn out all right, Mr. Lawson," Tully said. "The governor of this state was raised in an orphanage."

"That's how I was raised. In an orphanage. But I'll bet it was a lot worse'n orphanage than the one he was in."

Tully supposed there was something to all of this "advantages" talk that the Eastern newspapers were always discussing. Inevitably, it spread out here, where it met a much more skeptical eye. Tully supposed, as he usually supposed, that there was a middle ground that hit the subject just about right.

It was a lot tougher to grow up poor than to grow up in decent circumstances. But that didn't mean you had to *stay* poor the rest of your life, and that also didn't mean you had the moral right to commit crimes just because you'd been disadvantaged.

Which is what Bert Lawson here was sort of saying.

"Anything I ever stole, I figure it was just something society owed me."

"If we all thought like that, Mr. Lawson, we wouldn't have any society at all."

Lawson shrugged. "You're law. I wouldn't expect you to understand."

There was a supply room in the back Tully used to question prisoners. It was quiet and isolated. It was a good place to talk. The wisest man he'd ever deputied under had taught him that talk—prolonged talk—was a more effective weapon than pistol-whipping. Tully didn't have the knack—or the stomach—for torture, anyway.

Lawson was a slender man in the shabby clothes of a 'bo. He was cleaner than the average 'bo and had the easy insolence of the professional criminal in his blue eyes.

"I want you to tell me about the night of Kate Tully's murder."

"That make you feel funny, Marshal? Talking about her like she wasn't your wife?"

"A little. But let's concentrate on you, not me. Tell me everything about that night."

"You're gonna hang this on me, aren't you?"

"I just want the truth."

"I told you the truth. We didn't kill her."

"I need a lot more than that. I need you to describe the whole night to me."

"We was just lightin' out of town was all when we seen your little house. And the windas lit up. We hadn't had much luck in town. Most folks in this burg don't like 'bos, that's for sure. A few sonsofbitchin 'bos kill a couple little girls—I'm talking about that thing in Montana a couple months ago, you know?—and we all get blamed. 'Oh, 'bos're this and 'bos're that' 'Hide yer wives and kids because the 'bos're comin'.' But I tell you, Marshal, there's good and bad 'bos just like there're good and bad people in every walk of life."

" 'I'm sure that's true, Mr. Lawson. But let's stick to the night of the murder."

"This really don't bother you? Talking about your wife gettin' killed and all?"

"That's for me to worry about, Mr. Lawson. Just tell me about the night you went to my place."

"Well, we was hungry, of course. There'd been a small 'bo jungle near that edge of town, but the railroad dicks run them off, see? So we didn't have no place to turn in that night. And like I said, we was hungry. Real hungry."

"So you get up to the house . . ."

"So we see the house and we figger maybe the missus of the place'll give us somethin' to eat. She's maybe got some stuff left over from supper, see?"

"All right. So you go up to the door . . ."

"Well, all the lights are on. So we just naturally figured somebody was home. We go around back. That's what people expect 'bos to do. Like niggers. Not good enough to come to the front door."

"So you go around back and what happens?"

"Nothin'. Which is what we thought was strange. The back door was open, and all the lights was on. But we didn't hear nobody movin' around in there."

Only now did the full stench of Lawson reach Tully. Made the lawman sit up as if he'd been bit by a skeeter. How you snap to attention at a skeeter bite and try to find the little sumbitch.

Tully's head angled back as he continued talking.

"So tell me what you found."

"We, uh, found your wife."

"She was where?"

"Where? On the floor. And dead."

"You're sure she was dead?"

"Sure I'm sure. I seen enough dead people in my time, believe me. I was in the war, and there was dead people everywhere.

"So she's on the floor dead, as you say. Then what did you do?"

"Conners started taking stuff."

"Meaning you didn't?"

"I took a little bit of stuff."

Tully didn't believe him. Not that it mattered. The concern here was murder, not robbery.

"How'd Conners get blood all over him?

"I'm not comfortable sayin', Marshal."

"Say anyway."

"I'm tryin' to spare your feelings."

"Don't worry about my feelings."

Lawson rubbed a hand across a beard-stubbled face. Hard to say which was dirtiest, hand or jaw.

"He slipped in the blood. The blood on the floor. I never seen so much blood."

"And it got all over him?"

"You ever slipped in a pool of blood? He fell facedown, got it all over his coat and hands. And he banged his head pretty good, too. Put his fingers up there to feel the bump and even got blood in his hair."

"Then what?"

"Then we run. What would you a done? We run for the tracks."

"How'd the posse find you?"

"We was gonna wait for the train. Little gully there. I took off runnin'. Figured it'd be better if we split up for a while. Conners was still sort of woozy from hittin' his head."

"What you're saying is you deserted him."

"He woulda done the same thing."

"I want to go back to the house," Tully said. "Did you

ever have the sense that somebody might be hiding in there while you were there?"

"No, guess it didn't cross my mind. Figured you kill somebody like that, you'd run away."

"You hear anybody or see anybody on your way in or out—anybody near the timber there or on the hill to the east?"

"Heard a horse."

Tully's head snapped up straight. "A horse? Where?"

"In the timber somewhere."

"You sure it was a horse?"

"I been around plenty of horses, Marshal. And this sounded like a horse in some kind've pain or something. You know how they sound."

He was just about to ask more questions when somebody knocked on the door. Tully's mind was alive with all sorts of new possibilities. A horse in the timber. An injured horse. He'd combed the woods for anything that might've been dropped on the ground. But now he'd look for an entirely new kind of evidence.

"You just set right there," he said.

"You think I'm gonna get up and fly away?"

Oh, he was a treat, Lawson was. A real treat.

Tully opened the door to find Mack Byrnes standing there.

"Hate to tell you this, Marshal."

"Oh, shit."

Byrnes, looking sad, said, "The doc just sent somebody over with the news. Nan Conners died about fifteen minutes ago."

# PART FOUR

# ONE

DOC DALY HAD been in the room with her when she died.

He heard this deep sigh—one of utter exhaustion—and turned to look at her because he recognized the sigh for what it was. A sigh of resignation. A sigh of handing yourself over to the waiting darkness.

The doc had heard this particular sigh many times in his long career.

There were people who put up magnificent, downright Napoleanic battles against death. You could drown them, hang them, shoot them, disembowel them, and somehow they still hung on.

Then there were people who you gave some bad medical news and they just went home and laid down and died. Didn't fight at all. Took your medical news as a death sentence. He'd always suspected that these people *wanted* to die.

The little gal here, she'd sort of confused him.

She'd put up a good fight all night long but when he'd come back to the office just after dawn, she was slipping badly. He didn't sense, *feel* any kind of struggle in her. Her body was simply accepting its fate. Reva had sensed it, too. She couldn't understand why the girl had fought so hard in the first few hours and then seemed to give up. All Reva could figure out was that it had to do with the girl's brother. That kind of sorrow would weigh on a person, make her want to escape this vale of tears.

Nan Conners died at 10:57 A.M., according to the doc's railroad watch.

He asked one of his waiting patients—he had a houseful this morning, coughing, sneezing, and wheezing with colds and flu and allergies—to run and get the marshal and bring him back here.

He had a funny feeling that the marshal had gotten himself attached to the little gal. She'd been a sweet little thing, no doubt about that.

The patient, a cough-addled, hefty young man of sixteen, ran to the marshal's office. The doc hadn't told him about Nan. Figured that would be a terrible way for Tully to find out about her dying. That's how the doc had found out about his youngest daughter dying. Man coming into town —man he'd never even laid eyes on before—said, "Say, you're the doc what lost his daughter, I sure am sorry to hear that." And he then informed the doc that Lucinda had been crushed when her horse fell on her.

That wasn't the way you should learn about death, from some stranger like that.

The doc tended to his patients and waited for Tully to show up.

Tully had sure had a lot of grief lately.

People waved and said hello, but Tully didn't hear them. A wagon damned near ran him down, but he didn't hear it. A couple kids ran in front of him and shot him with wooden pistols, but he didn't fall dead. There wasn't any need. He was already dead.

He walked on instinct, didn't look, didn't hear, was completely turned inward. She'd been a damned good young woman and he'd responded to that. He still loved Kate—not even the leering Langley with all his filthy truths could kill his love—but he'd responded to Nan in a way that might have led to a different kind of love. And he'd known that almost immediately. She'd been as strong as Kate but not as willful and not as given to secrets. She was what she seemed to be, and you could accept that or move on. And he'd felt protective of her in the same way he'd felt of Kate when she went through the heartbreak following the miscarriage. He wanted a woman he had to take care of sometimes—and a woman who wouldn't mind taking care of him when the time came.

There was a small crowd around the front of Daly's office. This was a different group than the ones who'd turned out for the lynching. An older, more responsible crowd.

"We're back of you," a white-haired woman said. "If you want to go after Donnelly and Sieversen now, that's fine with us."

"They shouldn't have lynched that man," said the woman's slight husband. "And now they've gone and killed that poor girl. She was nice. We talked to her over to the park just yesterday afternoon.

"We're getting Cornelia Welles to sing at a special service for the Conners girl, Marshal," Father Flaherty said. "Least we could do."

"I appreciate it all, folks. But why don't you break up and go back about your business. Been too many crowds forming in town lately."

They recognized instantly what he meant. Crowds didn't usually form unless there was trouble. And there'd been too much trouble here lately.

He went inside.

Reva was just coming out of the operating room.

"She never woke up again, Marshal. I'm sorry."

"Yeah," he said. "So am I."

"Doc's in there now, if you want to go in."

Doc had a sheet over her. He stood with his back to Tully. He was filling out some kind of form. He smelled of whiskey.

"Sure hated to lose that one," he said.

"Yeah."

"Do me a favor and shoot the sonofabitch who killed her right on the spot. Don't bother with a trial. I sure as hell wouldn't, Tully, and that's no bullshit."

Tully walked over and started to lift the sheet.

Doc said, "Why you want to see her now? Remember her the way she was. Damned morticians're tryin' to convince everybody it's a good thing to see dead people, keepin' the caskets open and everything. Pile of crap, far as I'm concerned. Remember them the way they were. Soul's gone; they ain't human beings no more, anyway."

"Maybe you're right." Tully dropped the sheet back in place without looking.

The medical man finished up with his form. "You know anything about her kin?"

"I know where she lived. I can wire the sheriff there, see what he can turn up. Reva says you were with her when she passed?"

"She give a sweet little sigh. And that was that. She passed right then and there.

"She say anything?"

"Not that I could understand. She muttered from time to time, but I couldn't understand any of it. Probably about her brother. She sure was all pissed off about him." Then: "You got any idea who killed her?"

"None that I'd be willing to talk about right now," Tully said.

He put his hand on her shoulder. She was cold already. A great sadness came over him. So damned young. So damned worthwhile. A person with some real substance. He remembered the time he'd seen her sitting in church, her perky little hat and all, saying her rosary. He didn't know what to feel exactly. He wasn't especially sentimental about her. It wasn't that. It was just the unfairness of it all. Kate had died for no reason he could fathom, and now Nan had died for no reason, too. Something was going on in this town, something he needed to understand. And fast.

Reva peeked in. "You've got patients, Doctor." Daly nodded.

Reva glanced at the form beneath the sheet. "I'm sorry, Marshal."

After Reva closed the door, the doc said, "I meant what I said, Tully. You find the bastard who did this, shoot him right on the spot."

Tully said, "I'll keep that in mind."

May Kay Washburn was not a brave woman. She was afraid of heights, snakes, horses, storms, old age, Indians, colored people, Catholics, Jews, and at least seventy other categories of things and people.

So she surprised herself by putting on her nicest frock— she liked that Eastern word so much better than the plain, everyday word *dress*—and nicest picture hat and went over to the marshal's office after settling her nerves with a cup of tea.

There would no doubt be a reward for her exposing the jewel thief. And her picture would no doubt be in the newspaper. And all the people at the Methodist church would rush up and tell her how brave she'd been, living right there with him in her boardinghouse—an actor and a thief and God alone knew what else—right there in her very own home.

It was thrilling to think of herself as brave. Her mother and father had been brave, and her six brothers and sisters had been so brave they'd been foolish. But Mary Kay had never been brave. Until now. Until just this very moment.

She had been in the marshal's office once in the past ten years, to bring Marshal Tully the pie her church group had made for him. Tully had agreed, somewhat reluctantly, to come and talk to her group about law enforcement in the West and some of the new things going on where that was concerned.

Only Mrs. Henshaw disliked Tully's talk. "I thought he was going to talk about Black Bart and Jesse James and people like that. All this nonsense about fingerprints and things like that. I wasn't the least bit interested."

But all the other women had been, so they'd baked Tully an apple pie, and Mary Kay Washburn had brought it to him at the office.

But memory played tricks. She remembered the place as quiet, orderly, and as pleasant as a jail facility could be.

Perhaps she'd been there at just the right time that long-ago day.

Because today was very different.

Four prisoners in handcuffs and leg irons were being led out the front door on their way to the courthouse. They were coarse, filthy men, and they spoke in a coarse and filthy language. And they spoke loud, taking great pleasure in the fact that they were offending her.

"Pipe down," said the jailer walking behind them with a nightstick, "there's a lady present."

"I don't see no lady," said one of the convicts, "lessen it's you."

Which got a hearty chuckle out of the other convicts. And when they had gone, and she was about to go up to the front desk and ask to see Marshal Tully, she heard a woman scream and begin sobbing. It was the wildest, most heart-breaking sobbing Mary Kay Washburn could ever remember hearing.

A Mexican woman was being led up the corridor from the jail in back.

"He's going back to prison, isn't he?"she said, still wailing. She was swollen and beautiful with child, very near term by the looks of it. She was a tiny thing with huge Madonna-like eyes. The deputy was Mack Byrnes, and at this moment he seemed more friend than lawman.

Byrnes had his arm around her, trying to console her. "He broke into that place, Juanita. I'm sorry. We don't have any choice. We caught him in there last night, and now we have to tell the judge.

"And I will have our baby, and he will be in prison again!"

"I'll ask the judge to go easy," Byrnes said, obviously lying, trying to say anything that would calm the young woman. "Maybe the judge'll take your condition into account."

For the first time the young woman, her face glazed with tears, paused in her sobbing and said, "Such a thing is possible? That the judge man would take my condition into account?"

"Yes, it's possible, Juanita."

He escorted her to the door. She really was lovely, elegant in her brown and slender way, earnest and pure, timeless and immortal in her grief over her foolish and reckless husband.

"You will say these things to the judge?"

"Yes, I will, Juanita,"

"And you will go to the back now, to the cell where my husband is, and tell him these things so he will have some hope?"

"I'll do that, yes, I will."

She took his massive hand in her tiny one. "You are a good man, Deputy Byrnes. I will say many prayers that you live a long and fruitful life."

"Thank you, Juanita. Thank you very much."

When she was gone, Mary Kay Washburn said, "Those Mexicans. There just isn't any hope for them."

He smiled. "Yes, if they could only be as good as we are, right?"

She blushed at the implicit criticism of her. "Well, I certainly didn't mean it that way. I'm as open-minded as the next person. It's just—"

"What can I do for you, Mrs. Washburn?"

"I'm here to see Marshal Tully."

" 'I'm afraid he's gone for a while. Is there something I can help you with?"

She supposed he would do. He was well regarded, Mack Byrnes. And she did have shopping and cleaning and laundry to do. She may as well get it over with.

"Is there some place we could speak privately?"she said.

• • •

Langley carried his bags up to his hotel room and settled in. From here, he could see the train depot. He hoped that by tomorrow at this time he would be on the platform and boarding the train that would take him out of this dozing little burg.

Before he went, though, he intended to get his hands on the rest of the proceeds from the Carter jewel robbery. Not long now, and the rest of it would be his. Not long now at all.

# TWO

THERE WAS ALWAYS a point now, when his cottage came into sight, when Tully wanted to turn back to town. Find a new place. Never see his old home ever again.

He imagined that in addition to all of Kate's blood there had also been a good deal of Kate screaming for help. Sometimes, late at night, he woke up abruptly, disoriented, sweating, imagining that ghost screams had summoned him.

But it was early afternoon, and there were no screams. The cottage looked kempt and homey in the sunlight. The well in back, the two small outbuildings, the narrow creek glinting in the sunbeams . . . a good life could be lived here. A good life had been lived here.

Not even Kate's deceit could spoil his memories. He'd loved her, and that was sufficient for him. She'd honored her wedding vows, and for that he'd always admire her.

But memories of Kate fought now with memories of Nan Conners. Funny that somebody you knew so slightly could be as vivid—in some ways more vivid— than somebody you'd known for years.

He rode to the timberland a tenth of a mile in back of his place, dismounted, and ground-tied his animal. If Lawson was telling the truth—and there was always the chance that a law-hating man like Lawson could be up to mischief—Tully had been looking for the wrong things in the woods. There was a narrow path that led to Tully's land. Many horses traveled it as a shortcut to a wide bend of creek where they took water. Too many hoof tracks to be helpful. Nor, from what he'd been able to see, had anybody dropped anything or torn anything that was helpful, either. And he'd been over the path three different times.

But if Lawson was right . . .

On narrow paths like this one, horses sometimes brushed broken branches that pierced them like swords. Easy to imagine, especially at nighttime, a horse injuring itself this way.

Pine and juniper; damp fallen leaves; mold and mud . . . the timberland was fragrant this afternoon. Tully worked the left side of the path for the first hour.

He found nothing useful. There were plenty of spearlike broken branches, but none of them showed any evidence of having pierced horse flesh. Or human flesh, for that matter. They were clean of stains.

He kept his eyes at the level where a horse was likely to be stabbed, roughly from the base of the neck on down.

A couple of times he paused to roll himself a cigarette and enjoy the taste of it in the clean outdoor wind. This time last year, Kate would have been making preparations for the big spring dance Pine City always held. She was one of the main attractions. As a youngster, he'd always had a fantasy of falling in love with a beautiful girl whose beauty only he recognized. That way, he wouldn't have competition; he hadn't had much faith in holding a girl. But Kate hadn't been that girl. She disrupted rooms simply by entering them.

At one point, a couple of young, pigtailed girls came by on a sleepy old mare. They rode bareback. The girl in back carried a water bucket. The girls were maybe twelve.

"Hi, Marshal," they said shyly, almost in unison.

"Afternoon, ladies."

"I'm Peg," said the blonde one.

"I'm Connie," said the dark-haired one.

"Now, you sure don't think I'd ever forget two pretty girls like you, do you?"

They giggled.

"How come you're on the trail here?" Connie said.

"Well, if I was to tell you, you'd probably say I was loco."

"You *can't* be loco, Marshal," Peg said, "your're the marshal."

"Well I sure do thank you for that vote of confidence."

"What's 'vote of confidence' mean, Marshal?" Connie asked.

"It means having faith in somebody. I'm saying thank you for not thinking I'm loco." He paused and smiled at them on their sweet-faced broken-down glue pot of a horse, two barefoot prairie girls in faded dresses literally sewn together with rags of various kinds. "You ever see a horse that got hurt when a tree branch stabbed him? You know, like a knife being pushed in him?"

"Sure," Peg said. "My pa had a horse like that. And ma had to stitch him up her ownself because the horse doc, he was gone off somewhere."

"That's right. Well, if you was to see the branch that did that, it'd have blood on it. And probably hair from the horse, too, sticking to it. That's what I'm looking for,"

Then an odd thing happened. They stopped talking to him and started whispering back and forth, cupping hands to ears. It was a serious and lengthy conversation. And then, abruptly, they were done.

"We decided to tell ya," Peg said, "though our folks'll switch our britches if they ever found out we did."

"Tell me what?"

They looked at each other. And damned if they didn't spend another minute whispering back and forth.

"We seen this man, Marshal." Peg's face flushed as she spoke.

"We're really gonna get it now, Peg," Connie said.

"Well, we *should* tell him. We really should."

"Then you tell him."

Connie glanced at her friend. "Our mas, they sent us to get water that night. Later'n usual. They always send us together, seein's how our farms are so close'n all. And they figger we can look out for each other."

"You said you saw a man?" He was trying to be patient. It was getting difficult.

"We seen a man, and he was havin' trouble with his horse. His horse was buckin' and thrashin', just like a bull at a rodeo, Marshal."

Peg got in. "The horse was hurt. You could tell by the way it cried."

"The man finally got the horse calmed down, and then he took off ridin'."

"Where was this?" Tully asked.

"Back up at the other end of the trail," Connie said.

"So he was coming from—"

"We figgered he was comin' from down around your house," Peg said.

"And we figgered he was ridin' hard, and that was how his horse got hurt like that. Like with the branch you was mention'n and all."

"So in the mornin' we came back, and we found it."

"Found what?"

"The branch. With the blood on it."

He wished Nan Conners was here to share this moment. A man riding hard from his cottage. His horse injured. A desperate gettaway.

So Bert Lawson had been telling the truth.

"You think you can find that branch and show me?" Tully said.

Mack Byrnes said, "So you're sure of what you're saying, Mrs. Washburn? You're sure you saw a canvas bag with the Carter name on it?"

Mary Kay Washburn didn't like his tone. Here a law-abiding, churchgoing and (let's face it) *attractive* middle-aged woman comes to the marshal's office to divulge what may very well be some of the most exciting information ever uttered within these walls, and how does the deputy respond?

With skepticism, that's how he responds. With superiority, that's how he responds. With a certain *amusement,* that's how he responds.

"I don't appreciate your tone, Deputy."

"My tone?"

"You don't believe me?"

"It's not that I don't believe you, Mrs. Washburn. It's just that I have to make sure of what you're saying."

"Which is another way of saying you don't believe me."

"People make mistakes. I make mistakes all the time."

"I'm sure you do." He surprised her by smiling.

"I left myself open for that one."

She said, rather formally, "I have a ninth-grade education; I have good eyesight. I was only a foot or two at most away from the canvas bag. And I'm very sure of what I saw."

"You make a good case."

"So what are you going to do about it?"

"I'm going to talk to the marshal, and then I imagine we'll go looking for Langley."

"He could be gone by then."

"As soon as we finish here, I'm going to send a man to check the hotels and the other boardinghouses. There hasn't been a train out of here yet today, and the only stage won't arrive for another two hours—unless it's six or seven hours late as usual. He could have taken a horse, but from how you described him, that seems unlikely, so I'd say we're pretty safe in thinking he's still in town here."

"And what if he's not? What if you let him slip away?"

"Then I guess I'll be the one held responsible."

"I'm not sure that's a satisfactory answer."

"It's the only answer I have for you, I'm afraid, Mrs. Washburn."

"My husband would never have let you slough me off this way."

"I'm not sloughing you off at all, Mrs. Washburn. I'm doing all I can to check out your story." He slid off the edge of the desk he'd been perched on and said, "Now I've got to find a man to check out all the places he might be staying. Good day, Mrs. Washburn."

She gave him an exquisite look at her bosom as she rose—freezing herself there for a moment as she felt her breasts strain against the cotton of her dress—but he was beyond even the powers of her sexual charm. He was likely a dud in bed.

She started to say something, but before she could form the words, he said, "Good day, Mrs. Washburn," and nodded in the direction of the door.

He didn't even escort her to the front of the building.


The mayor was clipping his fingernails. Fingernails weren't as much fun to clip as toenails—toenails could be something of a manly challenge, at least toenails as thick as his—but a mayor could hardly put a bare foot on the massive mayoral desk and clip away on a sunny day at 3:06 P.M.

Not hardly.

The office was standard issue for mayors. Plaques of every kind from every organization you'd ever and never heard of. According to them—and to the inscribed photographs ranked along the east wall the mayor here was a combination Abe Lincoln/Pope/Attila the Hun figure who had made Pine City a sparkling gem of a town—the sort of town so splendid, so modern, so elegant and lovely and quintessential to the world that the people of Paris, Berlin, and New York would stream in here if they'd been given only half a chance, merrily overlooking some of the outdoor latrines and the outhouses.

"Dammit, Merle," Captain Sieversen, late of the United States Army (and don't you forget it) said, "do you have to do this while we're having a serious discussion?"

"Do what?"

"Do what?" Sieversen snapped. "Sit there and clip your damned fingernails."

"It's distracting, Merle, is what it is," Ralph Donnelly

said. "We're trying to talk, and all your attention is on your fingernails."

The mayor looked up at them, his narrow, pockmarked face smiling now. "You gentlemen should take a lesson here. Be a little more fastidious about your *own* fingernails. One sign of being civilized is good grooming."

"Fuck grooming," Sieversen said. "What the hell're we going to do about the Conners girl? Maybe you've been so busy with your fingernails that you haven't heard. Somebody killed her."

"Oh, I heard all right," the mayor said. And just then he got good purchase on a nail, clipped off a chunk of it, and sent it flying into space.

All three of them watched its arc.

*Why, jes look at that little sumbitch fly through the air, will you?*

"There's one thing Mayor Merle Cryer stands for," Mayor Merle Cryer said, "and that's law and order." He was finished clipping his nails now and dropped the clipper in the top left-hand drawer of his desk, the same drawer where he kept his dirty pictures and pint of bourbon. "And that means that by sundown tonight, we're going to arrest somebody for that murder."

"Who?" Sieversen said.

"Anybody. You two decide. Somebody who can't squawk. Preferably somebody with no connections at all. No family, no job; a drifter, if we can find one."

"And why would a drifter have killed Nan Conners?" Donnelly said.

"Why? Why, because he was so impressed with our town—he had a sober moment or two and saw what sort of fix the town was in with her stirring up trouble—that he took it upon himself to kill her."

"What if nobody believes that?" Sieversen said.

"Then we go the other way."

"And that would be what, Merle?" Donnelly said.

"That would be rape. The drifter lusted for her. Panted for her. Drooled for her. And she, being an upright and moral young woman, wanted nothing to do with him. So, in his anger, he got himself a rifle and shot her to death."

"That one would work better for me," Donnelly said.

"Me, too," said Sieversen.

"Lusted, panted, drooled," the mayor said.

"Lusted and panted," Donnelly said, feeling optimistic for the first time since hearing of Nan Conners's death, an event he feared would bring the state investigator right back here.

"Don't forget drooled," Sieversen said. He looked happy, too.

"Drooled," said the mayor, "drooled is very important."

# THREE

A S IT TURNED out, the girls couldn't find the bloody branch at first, either.

They remembered that it was here, and then they remembered that it was there. And then they remembered it was—

The day was cooling, shadows spreading like night's blood spilled, when Peg suddenly remembered, "That rock! Remember, Connie, I tripped on that rock and fell into the branch."

"That's right. I clean forgot," Connie said.

Things moved quickly then. A lone branch wasn't easy to find—not unless it extended into the trail itself—but a rock right on the side of the trail—

They started their search for the rock.

Sunlight like today's always made him melancholy—it seemed to have its own look and even aroma—and as he walked the trail looking for the rock, he thought again of Kate and Nan. Strange he'd couple them together this way, and yet he knew that they each deserved so vivid a berth in his memory. They'd both managed to touch him, and in finding out who had killed them, maybe he could sort out his feelings. He tried not to think of Kate's betrayal; he tried not to think about what Nan could have meant to him someday.

The snapping of winter-dried leaves on the ground, the smoky smell in the surrounding hills, the lonely flight of hawks against the perfect blue sky. For one of the few times in his life, he gave in to all-out pity for himself. He was usually able to push it away, laugh it off. *Oh, yes, Tully you've really got it bad, you do. You've got your health, a good job, the respect of most of the town. Oh, yes, poor, poor Tully. What was it the nuns used to say? Save your pity for somebody who deserves it, the way God wants you to; don't waste it on somebody as lucky as yourself, young Tully.*

And remembering their words was usually enough to hold the worst of it at bay. Sometimes when he was in a particularly self-pitying mood, he'd even laugh out loud at himself, downright mock himself.

But right now he just felt lonely and confused and in bad need of finding the person or persons who had killed Kate and Nan. Then maybe he could go back to holding self-pity at bay.

Peg was way down the trail, near the edge of his own land, when she called out. "I found it!"

Connie, who had been searching at a point between them, started running. Soon after, Tully did the same. He was getting a bit of a belly, and he sure felt it when he tried a full-out run. Between cigarettes and sticking at the dinner table too long, he was losing all vestiges of youth.

Peg was pointing proudly to a rock the size and shape of a loaf of store-bought bread.

"This is where I tripped, and here's the branch."

And so it was.

There had been rain and snow in the months since Kate's murder. The leaves had fallen off, birds had pecked at branches everywhere, and wind and the air itself had faded the stain, too.

But the stain, faint as it was, was undeniable. The jut of broken branch would've hit an average horse just below the front of the neck.

He examined the branch more closely. A couple of horse hairs still clung to the branch. Long brown ones.

"That be a help to ya, Marshal?" Peg said.

"It sure is. Thank you very much, girls."

"Is there any kind of reward, Marshal?" Connie said.

"Well, now, I hadn't thought about that. A reward, huh?"

"People're always gettin' re-wards, Marshal," Peg said.

"Well, how about a reward . . ." He paused, teasing them. "You girls like licorice?"

They were predictably exultant.

"Like it? We love it!" Peg said.

He reached in his pocket and gave them some coins.

"We can get licorice *and* chocolate with this!" Connie said.

"Careful not to give yourself a stomachache. I used to do that. Eat so much candy I'd make myself sick."

"I ate myself sick on cheese one time, Marshal. I couldn't git out of bed 'til next day," Connie said.

"I ate myself sick on walnuts one time," Peg said. "My mom told me that I was gonna break out in walnuts—you know, big lumps all over my face and my body—and I believed her, too, and started cryin', and then it took her a long time to convince me she'd just been tryin' to spook me so's I wouldn't eat all them walnuts again like I did."

"Well, there you go," Tully said. "You girls be careful now."

"We will, Marshal!" they cried and ran back up the trail to where their horse was ground-tied.

Tully walked down to the edge of his land.

Easy to sneak up on the house from here, especially at night. Have your horse waiting for you on the trail. Ride away fast when you heard those two 'bos coming.

Given everything he knew now about Kate, he wondered if her killer had also been her lover. He hadn't considered that before.

He'd considered the possibility that the 'bos had killed her, that Langley had killed her, that one of his own enemies had killed her.

But he hadn't considered the notion that she might be seeing somebody from Pine City, and that that someone had come out here to kill her. Maybe she was trying to break it off, and the lover got angry. Or maybe the lover was trying to break it off, and she threatened to tell somebody about their affair. Or maybe they'd just had some kind of lovers quarrel that had gotten crazy. As a lawman, he'd seen things like that happen many, many times. Two otherwise sane, sober people, and then a bad argument, a momentary lapse of judgment or sanity or whatever you wanted to call it—

Just a momentary lapse was all it took.

And one of you was dead.

All of a sudden, Langley was on his mind. Langley and the livery stable.

Dunston, who ran the livery, was a taciturn old fart who made a point of never listening to or carrying gossip. His predecessor, another old fart named Withers, had carried a story about a local merchant. The story happened to be false, and the merchant took great and abiding umbrage at it being repeated and passed on. He systemically began telling stories about Withers. So many stories, and so vile, and repeated so often, that local people who had known Withers for years and should have known better began to believe them. And so Withers eventually became, in the community eye, not merely a crusty old bastard . . . it was a town *filled* with crusty old bastards and nobody gave them a thought— but somebody who should not be around children, virtuous women, or even animals. Withers died of a heart attack one day. Just dropped down dead. And people did not have to wonder why. His business had dropped more than 50 percent, and his new competitor down the street—*another* COB (crusty old bastard) but one who was downright cuddly compared to the Withers of recent gossip—his new competitor was prospering. Withers, it was said, died of a broken heart.

Thus, there would be no gossip for Dunston, not even when the request for such was official and coming from a duly sworn lawman.

"You know who Langley is?"

"Reckon I could know, Marshal."

"Does that mean you do or you don t?"

"Ain't sure."

A deep, exasperated sigh. "Dunston, listen, this is important. And whichever way you answer, you aren't going to get in any trouble with anybody."

"You remember Withers?"

"I remember Withers."

"And what happened to him?"

"And what happened to him. But Dunston, this isn't the same thing."

"No? You're askin' me to talk about somebody when it ain't no business of mine." Dunston had frog eyes and a billy-goat goatee. He had store-bought teeth that whistled and skinny fingers so brown from chewing tobacco they looked as if he dunked them regularly in a dung heap.

"It may not be *your* business, but it's the town business, Dunston. Now, did he or didn't he get a horse here on the night I asked you about?"

"He could've."

Tully almost smiled. "A lot of people *could've*, Dunston. The question is, did he?"

"What if I said I don't remember?"

"Then I'd tell you to go look at your record books."

Dunston's eyes narrowed, as if he were considering a revolutionary new thought. "Hmm."

"Hmm what?"

"Can you *order* me t'do things, Marshal?"

"Sure. In some cases, I can."

"Could you order me to look this up in my books?"

"Yep."

"Then if you ordered me to, I wouldn't have no choice, right?"

Tully laughed. "Go look in your books, Dunston, and hurry up about it. And if anybody asks, I ordered you to."

"Could we say you ordered me to at the point of a gun?"

"Sure, if that'd make you feel better."

"Well, it'd make for a better story, if nothing else."

He went away.

The livery was busy at day's end. Dunston's three employees were saddling horses, dusting off buggies, getting stalls cleaned out for animals that would be boarded here tonight. The smells were the sweet-sour variety you expected around horses. Fresh hay was the sweetest scent of all.

Tully stood just inside the open barn doors, watching the street traffic. His next stop would be the vet's place down the street.

Dunston came back holding a stiff-covered accounting book.

Instead of giving Tully his answer, he simply handed Tully the book.

"Look on page thirty-six."

"You could save us both some time by just telling me."

"I ain't telling you nothing. And that's just what I'd say to anybody who asked. I didn't tell him nothing, and here he was holding a gun on me."

Tully smiled, shook his head, opened the book.

"Page thirty-six, Marshal."

"Right. I heard you the first time."

He opened the book to page thirty-six. Ran his finger down the lines of the day's transactions 'til he came to the horse Langley had paid for late that afternoon. So just where had Langley gone with the horse?

"Was that horse all right when he brought it back?"

"Far as I know. Why?"

"Wasn't injured or anything?"

"None of the boys mentioned it was."

He handed back Dunston's book.

Tully said, "Why don't I shoot you in the arm?"

"What?" Dunston's froggy eyes frogged even more. "What the hell you talking about?"

"You said it'd make a better story if I was holdin' a gun on you. Make an even *better* story if I'd shot you in the arm."

Dunston finally got the joke. "Real funny, Marshal. Real, real funny."

The vet was winding down for the day. He worked out of a small white barn near the wagon wheel factory. Nothing formal. You just brought in your animal and told Ernie Tummler what was wrong with it. Tummler was short, broad, muscular, bald, and blind in his right eye. He wore a pirate's patch over it, which made him something of an exotic figure to all the kids in town.

He was putting some salve on a fierce gray tomcat that kept hissing and spitting at him. The tomcat was missing a chunk of fur on his right hindquarters. The bare skin was bloody and raw.

Tummler held him down with a massive left hand. He was the descendent of Russian Jews who'd done some wrestling for shows back in New York.

"Sidney here was a very stupid boy last night, Marshal," he said, as Tully approached the table on which Tummler was working.

Sidney was Tummler's own cat. Sidney would look good in an eye patch, too. He had that piratical air about him.

"Out drinking and chasing women again?"

"Even stupider than that, Marshal. Took on a raccoon."

"He was pretty stupid."

"Raccoons look so cute and sweet. Cats must think so, too, because they're always tangling with them and always losing."

Tummler finished with the ointment, lifted his large hand from the back of the tom. Sidney sailed off the table and disappeared into the dusk-shadowy barn.

"His namesake—my brother Sidney—is the same way. Always fighting wrestlers he can't beat. Greco-Roman wrestling is for young men. Swift young men. Sidney is fifty-three this year and still wrestling twenty-year-olds to prove his manhood. It's a good way to end up crippled or dead."

He put the lid on the ointment tin. "So how can I help you, Marshal?"

"Late last fall . . . months ago, now. You remember stitching up a horse that had run into a broken branch?"

"Not offhand. I could look at my records."

"Would you mind?"

"It's no problem, Marshal. Meanwhile, you can look at all my friends."

Near the back of the barn were the injured and sick ones, Stacks of cages, some big, some small. Dogs, cats, birds, even a couple of pet frogs. The ones that weren't going to pull through looked beaten and sad and made you feel beaten and sad. The ones getting healthy had a confined air about them. They wanted to burst free the way Sidney just had.

He talked to the cats and dogs. Them, he was conversant with and had been most of his life. The frogs were another matter. Exactly how did you address a frog? How did you tell girl frogs from boy frogs?

He was contemplating such matters when Ernie Tummler came back.

"You know what?"

"What?"

"I am remembering now where I was during this time. In the state capital. A famous rabbi was speaking there. One from the old country. My wife wanted to see him, so we took the train down. Ole Doctor O'Shea—he retired before you even moved here—he always takes over for me. Says he likes to keep his hand in. Sidney likes him because he always gives Sidney chicken parts. The old doctor raises chickens now. Sidney loves when I go out of town."

"So I could ask O'Shea?"

"You could if he wasn't in the hospital. He had a heart attack last week."

Tully remembered hearing that. O'Shea, like Tummler, was a beloved figure. A man can't go wrong taking care of people's pets.

"Maybe I'll go over and see how he's doing," Tully said.

"I've been there four times already. Tell him Sidney sends his love. One thing, though."

"What?"

"His memory." Tummler tapped his skull. "It ain't the best."

# FOUR

"HE'S HERE," DEPUTY Steve Kepler said.
"Who's here?"
"In your office."
Tully had hired young Kepler because young Kepler was unflappable. But at the moment he was most definitely flappable.
"Steve. Calm down and tell me what the hell's going on."
"The mayor."
"All right."
"In your office."
"All right. Anything else?"
Young Kepler looked sweaty, sick. "Sieversen's with him, and they're talking about—" He stopped, gulped. He was flapped, definitely flapped, over whatever the hell was going on here.
"They're talking about firing you, Marshal."
"Well, I'll just have to go in and talk to them, won t I?"
"If they fire you, I'll quit."
"You don't have to do that, Steve."
"Sure, we've got a baby on the way—"
"Steve, listen—"

"And sure, we've got some debts—"

"Steve, please—"

"And sure, the doc says the youngest girl's gonna need some eyeglasses pretty soon and—"

Tully patted Kepler gently on the arm. "You don't have to quit, Steve. So relax."

"It would be kind of a hardship—"

"They aren't going to fire me."

"They aren't?"

"They can't afford to. That'd be the fastest way to get the investigator from the state attorney's office back here."

"It would?"

"It would. Now, you just relax and think about all the reasons you can't afford to quit."

"So you wouldn't be mad if I didn't quit? I mean, even if they did happen to fire you?"

"No, I wouldn't be mad, Steve. In your position, I wouldn't quit, either."

"You wouldn't?"

"Nope."

"You sure made me feel better, Marshal. Thanks."

Young Kepler looked even younger just then.

Tully went on into his office.

Langley had a daughter somewhere back in Ohio, and for some reason, as he stood at the bar in Donnelly's casino, he thought about her, something he rarely did.

He supposed he was thinking of his own immortality. Fathering a child—propagating the species—was about the only thing he'd ever done to qualify him for that particular distinction.

The voices, smoke, laughter, and noise of the various gambling devices suddenly seemed furious to him. Louder and louder it got as he stood at the bar, drinking his good bourbon. And in the center of all that fury was emptiness. An emptiness reflective of his whole life.

He was a bullshitter of the first rank and could usually bullshit everybody—including himself—into believing just about everything.

But two, three times a year, a vexing gray moment enveloped him, and he was called by some unseen force to give an accounting of himself. And the accounting was always miserable. And always led to the same thing: a pledge to do something useful with his life.

Tonight's pledge ran thus: he would get the rest of the Carter jewelry proceeds, and he would head east, pausing long enough in Ohio to see his daughter. She would be eleven now. He wondered if she were pretty. But how could she not be, coming from him and a very pretty farm girl who had been positively delighted to let a New York actor take her virginity?

The pregnancy had forced her to flee—in shame—from her small farming community to Cleveland, where she married a much older widower who had agreed to adopt her child if she agreed to be his faithful wife. In her letters to Langley—which always came to him through his theatrical agent—she was careful to speak only kind words about her husband. He seemed to be a decent fellow: tender mate, exemplary father. Just rather stuffy and dull.

She also talked about how much she still loved Langley and how she still had dreams of their three nights of lovemaking. She said that no man would ever be able to bring her to such passion ever again, not even the young ones she'd started sneaking off with, much to her shame. She said she prayed every night for strength to leave the plucky young ones alone but couldn't. She snuck out by moonlight and trysted down by a nearby coal yard, Cleveland being the industrial titan it was, coal yards everywhere.

He had no interest in her. She'd been dull of mien and dull of sex the nights he'd spent with her. But their child—he was sure the girl was blonde and golden and possessed of his own charm and intelligence. He just wanted to see her. Just once. Didn't even need to speak with her. Just seeing her would be enough.

He finished his drink and ordered another.

By tonight, the rest of the Carter proceeds would be his, and by morning, he would be on the train. And forty-eight hours hence—well, all right, at least fifty-six hours hence, given how trains honored their schedules—he would be in Cleveland, glimpsing his daughter.

One way or another, he was going to see her.

Impatiently, he checked his railroad watch again.

He wanted to get the rest of the loot and have it over with.

"And this paper here is what exactly?" Tully said.

"Your resignation," Sieversen said.

"I see. And why exactly are you forcing me to resign?"

"For the good of the community, Tully," the mayor said. "It's nothing personal."

"No, of course not. Firing people is never personal."

"You know very well what I'm saying," the mayor said. "You've been an excellent marshal. and you know it. In fact, I consider you a friend,"

Tully spared the man a laugh. They'd never liked each other.

Tully went behind his desk and sat down.

He said, "So, who killed Nan Conners?"

"What's that got to do with anything?" Sieversen said.

Tully rolled himself a cigarette. "You don't want me to find out who really killed my wife. Because if I find out and the killer didn't happen to be Francis Conners, you're all in a lot of trouble. You killed an innocent man. And that one you just might be able to get away with. But then you're still stuck with who killed Nan Conners. Francis Conners couldn't have killed his own sister, because you'd already killed *him*."

"That's where you're wrong, Tully," Sieversen said. "We know who killed Nan Conners."

Tully allowed himself to smile.

"And who would that be?"

"A drifter name Theodore Wilkinson," the mayor said.

"I see. And how did you find this out?"

"He was found drunk on grain alcohol down by the rail yards," Sieversen said. "Babbling and out of his mind. Vomiting blood. The yard man who found him took him to the hospital. When he started sobering up, he told a nurse about the Conners woman."

"You have a niece who's a nurse there, don't you, Sieversen?"

"Yes. Sally.

"And I'll just bet it was Sally he told this to, wasn't it?"

"Yes, it was, as a matter of fact. And keep your damned suspicions to yourself. She's a reputable young lady."

They'd thought it all out very well. He admired their cleverness if not their scruples.

"And where is this drifter now?" Tully said.

"He's your only prisoner at the moment. We brought him in an hour ago.

"Kepler didn't mention anything about a prisoner."

"Kepler," Sieversen said, "didn't know anything about it. The mayor and I brought him in the back way. Why don't we go back and talk to him, Tully? He's willing to tell you everything."

Tully shook his head, knowing they were preparing him for yet another surprise. They must have something up their sleeves, or else they'd just be trying to escort him out of here, fast as possible. They were good at what they did but not subtle.

They trooped back to the four cells in the rear of the building.

Tully wasn't all that surprised to find a man hanging from the barred window above him, dead by strangulation. He had apparently hanged himself with his own belt.

"Oh, my God," said the mayor in utter surprise.

"This is terrible," said Captain Sieversen, late of the United States Army.

"I take it this is Theodore Wilkinson," Tully said.

"I should've remembered to take his belt from him," Sieversen said.

Tully said, "Now I'll never get a chance to talk to him, will I? I guess I'll just have to take your niece's word for it that he confessed to killing Nan Conners, won't I?"

"I'm afraid so," Sieversen said. "Yes, indeed, I'm afraid so."

# PART FIVE

# ONE

THEY FOLLOWED TULLY back to his office. He went behind his desk, sat down, took up his pen, signed the resignation, folded it twice, and set it on the desk.

He took off his badge and laid it on top of the resignation.

"I'm sorry it's come to this, Tully," the mayor said.

Tully had said nothing since leaving the cell. He said nothing now.

He stood up, went over and picked up his hat from the top of a small bookcase, and walked out of the office.

"Aren't you even going to say good-bye, Tully?" Sieversen called after him. "Aren't you even going to say good-bye?"

The hospital was one-story white clapboard with ten beds.

Suppertime. Smells of good food, clatter of pans and dishes and silverware. Laughter and greetings. The only festive moment in the otherwise slogging day of the hospital. The food smells hid the medical smells, which made things even nicer.

He found O'Shea, the ancient animal doctor, in a small

two-bed room near the back of the place. So far, Tully had eluded all the nurses.

Somebody had left a tray of food on O'Shea's nightstand, but he wasn't eating. He was snoring. He was little more than a skeleton, pale, papery flesh draped loosely over sharp bone. He might've been two hundred years old the way he looked and the way he smelled of cruel time and even crueler decay.

He lay on his back, hands folded upon his stomach, coffin-ready. His snoring was almost musical because of the way, every so often, it whistled.

Directly across from him the other patient, a heavyset, ruddy-faced man, was also snoring, but there was no art or music to it. It was like lip-farting.

Tully leaned over and whispered to O'Shea, "Doc, I need to ask you a question."

But O'Shea didn't respond in any way except to keep on snoring and occasionally whistling.

"Doc. Please, Doc, wake up."

If he could speak out loud, he could probably stir the old man.

"Doc, please, wake up."

"Did you want to speak to the doctor, Marshal?"

A high, flutelike voice, not unpleasant. A tall, severe looking nurse whose severity vanished when she smiled. "He's a chore to wake up. But he should wake up and eat, anyway. Here, let me try."

Rustle of white garment. Long, efficient fingers put upon the old man's shoulder. Bob of white cap and she said, "You need to eat your supper, Doctor O'Shea, or the marshal here will arrest you."

O Shea's eyelids flung wide, and for just a moment his blue eyes were innocent as an infant's as his mind tried to comprehend who he was, where he was, and exactly what he was doing here in this body.

"What's for supper?" he said weakly.

"Broth."

"Again? I want meat and potatoes."

"The doctor said broth for supper."

"What the hell's he know? Young pup like him."

Then O'Shea saw Tully. "You here to arrest me?"

Tully laughed. "Something like that." He was glad he didn't have to take care of an oldster this cranky. "I need to ask you a couple of questions."

"Tell her to get me meat and potatoes."

"I don't hold any sway in the hospital, I'm afraid."

"Use your gun, then. Go back there and get me some meat and potatoes at gunpoint."

"He's such a pleasure to take care of," the nurse said, lifting the bowl of broth to his lips and filling a spoon.

"She don't mean that, Tully. She thinks I'm a pain in the you know where."

"Hard to believe anybody'd think that about *you*," Tully said.

"You're as sarcastic as she is." He let her spoon some broth into his mouth. "Acck. That stuff tastes like sheep piss."

"The doctor here must've drunk a lot of sheep piss in his time," the nurse said. "He seems to know exactly what it tastes like."

"See how sarcastic she is?" the old man said.

"She likes you, Doctor," Tully said. "She just has a hard time admitting it to herself."

The nurse smiled. "That must be it." She forced some more broth down him. He made a horrible face. No wee one eating vegetables had ever made one more horrible.

"The last time you filled in for the vet," Tully said.

"Yeah, what about it?"

"You treated a horse that'd been cut in the neck or chest,"

"I did?"

"That's what your records say."

The nurse rammed another spoonful home.

"Shoot her, Marshal," O'Shea said. "You have my permission."

The nurse giggled. Readied another spoonful. O'Shea

made another spectacular face when he saw the spoon coming at him.

Tully waited 'til the nurse had finished persecuting the old man with his latest dose.

"So what if I did?" O'Shea said.

"I was wondering if you remembered whose horse it was."

"Now how the hell would I remember that? That was a long time ago."

"I wish you'd think about it. It'd help really help me out."

The nurse started to push a another spoonful toward O'Shea, but he put a hand up and pushed the spoon back a few inches. He looked thoughtful. "Seems like I do remember something like that."

"Would've been a branch. Like a stab wound."

"Yeah, I do sort of remember treatin' it. But who the hell did the horse belong to?"

"What're *you* doing here, Tully?"

He turned to see Sally Dobbins—formerly Sally Sieversen, niece of the town's self-described "most distinguished soldier" (they'd made him delete "warrior" in the speech he'd written about himself)—who ran the hospital at night. She was a skinny, dour woman with hard, dark eyes and a frown that made strong men quake.

"I'm here seeing the doctor."

"He a friend of yours, is he?"

"He's here on business," O'Shea said, "marshal business."

"Well, that's awfully strange," she said, "since he isn't marshal anymore."

"What's that supposed to mean?" O'Shea said.

"He resigned—before they could fire him."

"He wasn't doing anything wrong," the other nurse said.

"You go take care of room B," Sally Dobbins said. "You're going to get written up for not telling me that Tully was here."

"He's the marshal. Or was."

"You should've told me, anyway. Now get over to room B."

The nurse looked embarrassed and angry. Tully felt sorry for her. Over the years, he'd had his share of drubbings from angry bosses in front of others. Nothing was quite as humiliating as that particular form of social punishment. Made you feel helpless, like a child.

"As for you, Tully, I want you to leave."

"Are visiting hours over?"

"They are for you."

"Say," O'Shea said, "I don't like the way you're treatin' him."

"You should thank me then," Sally Dobbins said. "It gives you something new to complain about."

She grabbed Tully's elbow. She had a good grip. She gave off a sharp odor of sweat. Her white uniform was stained under the armpits.

Tully didn't budge.

"You heard what I said, Tully. Out."

"Your uncle give the order, did he?"

"My uncle didn't *have* to give the order. I haven't liked you since you brought that woman back here with you. The way all the men stumbled all over themselves when she was around. Treated her like some sort of royalty." She smirked, "But I guess we know what she really was by now, don't we, Tully?"

A man, you could hit. A woman . . . he wasn't a wit or a word man. He rarely had the snappy rejoinders you heard on the stage.

"She was a decent woman," he said, knowing how ineffectual he sounded.

"Sure she was, Tully," Sally Dobbins said. "Sure she was. Now I want you out of here."

O Shea said, "I want you to tell my doctor that this broth tastes like sheep piss."

He'd already forgotten the question Tully had asked him.

Just at dusk, Mary Kay Washburn was coming home from the general store.

She'd forgotten to get a can of condensed milk for the

special way she fixed creamed corn. She liked the town at this time of night, the stars just beginning to burn through the cloth of bruised blue sky, a streak of late winter white, red, and yellow on the northeast horizon, and that fresh chill that seemed to revive every ounce of blood in your body. And that was how she came to see him.

Swaggering out of his hotel as if he owned the town. Langley.

Her first thought was to go over and start pounding on him the way you would a bully. She would never be able to forgive or forget his hurtful words of last night. That was her first thought. He was a thief—or perhaps far worse—but her primary reason for despising him was because he'd said all those horrible things to her. Things at least a part of her mind accepted as true.

She stopped, watching him head toward the block of saloons.

And then she wondered, *Why isn't this man behind bars? Why hasn't he been arrested for taking all the loot that poor Mr. Carter had had with him on the stagecoach?*

That had been her best weapon. Going to the law. Informing on Langley.

But apparently, it had done no good.

Here was Langley swaggering about as usual.

What kind of town was this, anyway?

His mocking words came back to her.

There didn't seem to be any hope of avenging herself on this man.

No hope at all,

# TWO

TULLY FIGURED MACK Byrnes would come looking for him, and he was right. Tully made it easy for his friend. He stood at the bar in his usual saloon, working slow on a couple of beers.

The regulars still didn't know how to treat him, They'd always paid him deference when he was a lawman. They'd been doing that for a lot of years. Wasn't easy to just stop. But now, if they'd wanted to, they could've just come up and picked a fight with him, and there wasn't a damned thing he could do about it. Not officially. There were a lot of people Tully had arrested in his time, and most of them knew that Tully wasn't an especially tough man. He was a good lawman—organized, up to date, reasonably fair—but that didn't make him tough. If he stuck around long enough, the beer and whiskey flowing, somebody was bound to give it a try.

He watched in the mirror behind the bar as Mack came in through the batwings. Several of the drinkers congratulated him on his new job as marshal. Mack looked uncomfortable. He wore the same old badge, the same old gun, the same old clothes. Mack wasn't the sort to make a fuss.

When he saw Tully, he kind of ducked his head, shy, and then slowly came over and stood next to him. He nodded to the sleeve-gartered man behind the bar. The man knew what he wanted. Tully and Mack Byrnes had spent a fair number of hours in this place.

"It's a hell of a way to get a promotion," Mack said, coming right to the point.

"You'll do a good job."

"I didn't have anything to do with forcing your hand,"

"Hell, Mack, I know that,"

"Donnelly, I can deal with. Sieversen, I'm not so sure." Mack looked around the saloon. Pinochle and poker were the games here. There was a player piano on a small bandstand where a fat, bad singer sometimes put on blackface.

"They're watchin' us," Mack said.

"I know."

"They think I helped push you out."

"Yeah."

"I'm hearing that everywhere." He sipped some of his newly arrived beer. Then coughed. He was famous for his sinus problems. All this smoke didn't help.

"They're hoping we get into a fight."

"You'd win."

"Hell, are you kidding, Mack? You'd knock me out in four or five punches. I saw you take on that prizefighter at the county fair."

"Maybe I got lucky."

"You know better than that. He was expecting a rube, and you took him apart."

Mack shrugged. "Well, we may've cleared up one thing today, anyway."

"What's that?"

"Mrs. Washburn who runs the boardinghouse?"

"Uh-huh."

"She claims that Langley fella robbed the stagecoach. Says she saw the Carter bag in Langley's room, anyway."

"Where's Langley now?"

"She came to the office about ten minutes ago and told me

I wasn't doing my job. With everything that happened today—with you and the mayor and all—I didn't have much time to look for him. She tells me she just saw him go in the Nugget. Guess I'll go on over there and talk to him.

Now came the difficult part for both of them. Tully said, "I'm going to keep looking, Mack."

"I sort of figured you would."

"They're not going to like it."

"I know. They told me to arrest you if you kept on questioning people."

"I don't want trouble, Mack."

"Neither do I."

"So what happens now?"

"I guess we'll just have to see."

"I hate this, Ben."

Tully nodded. Then: "Guess you'd better get over to the Nugget before Langley leaves town on you.

"What're *you* gonna do?"

"For tonight, not a damned thing except stand here and get just drunk enough to sleep for about ten hours. Then get up in the morning and see how I feel about things."

"Make it easy for me, Ben. Let me handle it. I'll find out what you want to know. I promise you."

"Watch yourself with Langley. He's pretty slick." The two men stared at each other for a time.

Mack Byrnes said, "Can I tell the family you'll be out for supper soon?"

"I'd like that, Mack. I really would."

Mack drained his beer, shrugged inside his shirt, and left.

One thing Langley did well was tell stories about the women he'd allegedly had sex with. And it was never ordinary sex. It was always dangerous sex. That's why there was always a small crowd around him along the bar as he intoned his triumphs.

He was particularly good with sneaking-out-of-rooms stories. These always involved married ladies. The men who listened had mixed feelings about these stories. On the one hand, they enjoyed them. He was one hell of a yarn spinner. Nobody was better at slinging the shit than a professional actor. But on the other hand, this was exactly the type of man they feared would be sniffing around their *own* wives. He was sleek, handsome, cunning: all the things his listeners were not. They could see their wives sneaking off with just such a fella, goddamn whores.

But beer made them forget their fears, and they gave in to his tales, alternately feeling terrified (here came the husband up the stairs), shocked (even with the husband just on the other side of the door, Langley wouldn't pull out until after he'd come), and greatly amused (there went Langley, jay-bird naked, hurling himself out a second-floor window). Was there a better beery way to spend a night than listening to such tales?

A number of men had drifted over to his part of the bar hoping to hear his usual war stories ("Tales of the Pussy" as he liked to call them) but he wasn't up for it. Oh, he was polite enough, but he was also subdued, something Langley rarely was.

"Buy you a beer, Mr. Langley?" one man after another asked, hoping for some entertainment. But Langley just shook his head no and said, "Think I'll turn in early. I'll be leaving town in the morning."

The men were like children who woke on Christmas morning to find that there were no gifts to be had. Santa Claus had apparently stayed in the North Pole with a bad head cold or something.

They could see that Langley was anxious about something. Way he kept checking his railroad watch. Way he kept grinding his jaw muscles. Way he kept frantically pushing his finger through the spilled beer on the bar.

This wasn't like Mr. Langley at all.

The chill on the late winter night sent the boarders up to their rooms a little earlier than usual.

Nine o clock was their normal time for heading up the stairs after saying good night to Mary Kay Washburn in her parlor—and getting some sleep for the next day ahead. Especially the railroad linemen, who worked exceptionally hard.

They were all in bed now, and she always felt good about that, like a mother who'd put her brood down, safe and sound for the night, and had a bit of free time on her hands. The night air was blessedly clear. She would sleep with the window cracked open, blissfully asleep under a fortress of covers.

She was drinking tea and reading a magazine when she heard the footsteps on her porch. She went to the window and peeked out through the heavy lace curtains.

A dark figure, familiar somehow, knocked on the door.

She didn't want him to wake her boarders. She hurried to the front door.

"I don't appreciate callers this late," she said, speaking to the phantom form she still could not see in any detail. A streetlamp at the far end of the street radiated muzzy yellow light, lending the fiery leaves a peculiar sand color. Somewhere a horse, pulling a buggy, clopped along the dirt street. And somewhere else a baby cried.

"It's not even eight o clock, Mrs. Washburn."

"This is a respectable place."

The black form sighed. Mary Kay Washburn could exasperate a saint.

"It's Ben Tully, Mrs. Washburn."

"I hear you're not marshal anymore, Mr. Tully."

"That's true, but I'd still like to talk to you."

"About what?"

"About Langley."

"We've talked about Mr. Langley."

"Has his room been rented?"

"Not yet. Why?"

"I'd like to see it."

"Why?"

"See if he left anything behind."

"Like what, Mr. Tully?"

"I don't know. That's just it. See if there's anything that

could help me." He sighed again. "I have to be honest with you, Mrs. Washburn. I don't have any official authority to do this."

"I'm aware of that, Mr. Tully. That's why I don't want to let you in. I don't want to get involved in whatever's going on."

"I think he may have killed my wife, Mrs. Washburn."

"I thought the man they hanged killed your wife."

"I'm not sure if that's the case."

"You really think Langley may have killed your wife?"

"Yes, ma am, I do."

Mary Kay Washburn had no trouble believing this. Any man who could say the cruel, hurtful things he'd said to her, any man who could tell such vicious lies, any man who could take such pleasure in undermining the self-confidence of a decent, even wonderful woman such as herself, well, if he was capable of saying what he'd said to her, then he was certainly capable of murdering a woman, wasn't he?

And if Ben Tully here was right, they would hang him. Give him just what he deserved for being such a foul-mouthed—

"You think you can prove this, Mr. Tully?"

"I hope to. I think he came to town here for two reasons. To rob the stagecoach and to see my wife."

To see his wife? My, how the juices flowed in Mary Kay Washburn. In addition to helping get Langley hanged, was she also going to learn the kind of gossip that would be shared for years to come?

"Well, I guess I shouldn't leave you standing out there in the cold now, should I?" she said.

She stepped back to let Tully come inside.

Tully spent an hour in the room where Langley had stayed.

Mary Kay Washburn stayed right there with him.

What did she think he was going to steal? he wondered. The bureau? Or maybe he'd strap the bed on his back and cart it downstairs.

She kept shushing him to talk more quietly whenever he

asked a question. Her boarders were trying to sleep. And she was a respectable woman. And this was a respectable house.

A couple of times his eyes paused at her bosom. It was quite the bosom, no doubt about that. But there was a sad, desperate look in her eyes whenever she caught him glancing at those splendid breasts of hers. She became—instinctively, it seemed, she'd reacted this way since she'd first sprouted them—she became coy. And she was too old and fat to be coy. She was like her house: once elegant and proud but now crumbling and pathetic. He felt sorry for her. He was sure he was just as pathetic in his own way.

He found nothing.

A full damned hour, opening drawers, peeking under the bed, crawling around in the closet, and nothing.

They went back downstairs, "Would you care for some apple cider?"

He wanted to say no, wanted to get out of there, but cider actually sounded good.

"Thanks."

They sat in the parlor.

He sat in a chair next to a small, doily-covered table upon which rested three framed photographs. She gave the history of each person. She spoke proudly of her walrus-mustached father, who had been a manufacturer's representative (she might have said salesman or even drummer, but then this was Mary Kay Washburn, wasn't it?) and affectionately of her mother ("the kindest, sweetest person I've ever known").

When she came to the lookalike middle-aged woman in the third photograph, tears took her voice and eyes. "We almost looked like twins. My sister Elaine and myself, I mean. She died of the cancer a year ago." Her voice was almost angry with tears now. "It should have been me. She was a much better woman than I'll ever be, Mr. Tully. She was like my mother. Really a very good person. Very unselfish and generous. She didn't suffer from my . . ." She hesitated. "Vanity, I guess you'd say. She didn't have my vanity at all. And when she was dying—I took the train to Elgin, Illinois, and stayed with her the last five weeks she was alive—she never complained or took it out on other people, you know how some dying people do." A sorrowful smile. "Lord, when my time comes, you won't want to be anywhere within two counties of me, I'll be feeling so sorry for myself and everything." She took a handkerchief from her sleeve, dabbed her eyes, and then blew her perfect little nose into it. "She was such a beautiful woman in every way, Mr. Tully."

So Mary Kay Washburn knew about herself, Tully thought. And punished herself. Every once in a while you start to like (or maybe forgive) somebody you'd previously disliked or even hated. You see something admirable or likable in them, and your feelings change. You look at them differently somehow, see their grief or burden, and you see that they're pretty much like you are, pretty much like *everybody* is. Sort of insecure, sort of awkward, sort of scared. And you can't dislike them anymore, even though you may want to.

"You would've liked her."

"I'm sure I would've, Mrs. Washburn."

"How's your cider?"

"Fine. I'm enjoying it."

"You know it can get stains out of certain things."

He smiled. "I'll have to remember that."

"I used cider on Langley's trousers, as a matter of fact."

"Langley's trousers?"

"The night he got into a fight in the backyard."

"One of the boarders?"

"No," she said. "Much as they wanted to take a poke at him sometimes. He can be a very arrogant man."

"Tell me more about the fight."

"I suppose it was one of his cronies from the saloon. He liked to walk home taking the alleys. Maybe he peeked in windows at women."

"Could be. But what about the fight?"

"Oh, it was the usual ruckus men make. Way back there, near the alley. Just two of them."

"Did they wake you up?"

"I was sitting up reading a magazine, and I heard it."

"Did you see them?"

"I came out the back door, and when the other man heard me, he ran away."

"Did you see him?"

She shook her head. "Too dark."

"Did Langley say anything?"

"He was too busy wiping his face. He had a terrible nosebleed."

"So he just came in the house?"

"He just came in the house and then he saw the grass stains on his new trousers. He was very upset about them. He asked me if there was any way I could get it out. He said he'd pay me."

"Did he ever say who he was fighting with?"

"No."

"Or why he was fighting?"

"No."

"Did you get the stains out?"

She tapped her glass and smiled. "Cider works every time, Mr. Tully."

# THREE

FRANK MET A man once—this was in Chicago, in one of those saloons he never told his brother Ralph about—who claimed he'd actually done it to himself with a nail, but the man was a liar, had to be a liar, because when pressed as to where he'd *put* the nail, the man got vague,

And you can bet Frank was careful to check out the man's palms.

Because where else would you put a nail?

You might put it through your wrist, though that would have to be one hell of a nail, and you might even put it through your foot, though that would have to be an even bigger nail.

What Frank was doing tonight was trying not to think about what he'd been thinking about all day.

It was funny, the way the alcohol worked on you. Sometimes you couldn't be sure what you'd actually done. Or what you were *afraid* you'd done. Or what you'd *wanted* to do but hadn't.

It was like a mystery. You searched your mind over and over again for clues, like in those British mystery stories he sometimes read.

Your mind knew the truth, but because of the alcohol, you couldn't be sure if it was *telling* you the truth or not.

But maybe there was a way of shocking your mind into a moment of absolute clarity. Punishing yourself so horrifically that you came, quite literally, to a moment of truth with your mind.

Same as with the razor and the cigarette burns. In punishing yourself, you learned what you'd really done.

He lay on the bed, smoking his cigarette, staring at the ceiling. He hadn't had a drink all day, and he was afraid he knew why.

Because tonight he was going to force himself to confront the truth and, whatever it was, he wanted to be sober for it.

He took his cigarette and guided it to his arm.

Stench of burning hair, burning flesh.

A soft cry, one of equal parts pain and pleasure.

Closing his eyes, letting the tears come. In joy and grief.

He wished he could explain to Ralph why he'd done this to himself all his life. Hell, he wished he could explain to *himself* why he'd done it.

Pulled the cigarette away.

Grasped the wounded arm.

The pain. The fucking pain.

There would be a lot more of it before this night was over.

But at least then, he'd know.

The tears continued to stream, and he began to shake. He wanted a woman to hold him, rock him, give him peace and darkness.

Peace and darkness . . . maybe they were the same thing.

Tully didn't actually see the shooting, but he heard it from two blocks away.

Walking back from Mrs. Washburn's. Sleepy, silent houses on both sides of the street. Perfect weather for sleeping deeply. Clean night air. Aroma of logs burning.

His mind jumbled with thoughts of many things. Pain now when he thought of Kate—so many things she'd kept from him. Loss when he thought of little Nan—so sweet and earnest. Anger that the town was determined to keep secret the identity of the real killer because they'd lynched the wrong one.

And then the shots.

Loud, sharp, quick.

For all his years as a lawman, Tully hadn't been around all that much gunfire. This was the era in the West when the lawyers and the courts had started to take over most disputes. The occasional cowboy might shoot up the occasional Saturday, or two hotheaded kin might muster a muzzle or two to shoot drunkenly and uselessly at each other, but a gunshot still had the power to startle and scare him. They almost always meant trouble; almost always serious trouble.

He had to remind himself, there in the middle of the shadowy, sleepy street, that he was no longer a lawman and that gunshots were no longer his province, unless of course they happened to be directed at him.

But he broke into a trot, anyway.

The crowd formed fast.

Batwings were flung wide and the men and women from the saloon started streaming down the stairs to try to figure out what had happened exactly.

Didn't take long. Whole thing was pretty self-explanatory.

Here you had, smoking six-shooter in hand, Mack Byrnes standing over the unmoving form of the actor Langley.

A derringer glinted in the moonlight, inches from the man's hand.

"What the hell happened, Marshal?" a drunk said.

Some of the people, who didn't know yet that Byrnes was now marshal, figured the drunk had just misspoken.

Byrnes looked somewhat dazed. He'd never killed anybody before, not even in the war.

"I was taking him back to jail—" He glanced at the faces. "You men from the Nugget saw me arrest him in there."

"We sure did, Marshal," one of the Nugget customers said, eager to agree.

"He didn't want to go. And finally I had to pull my gun."

"We seen it all, Marshal," another man said. "You done your best to bring him along peaceful."

"I should've thought of a derringer," Byrnes said.

"Fancy boys like him always carry 'em," a man said.

"Anyway," Byrnes said, shaking his head as if to clear it, "I got him out in the street here and was taking him over to jail, and he turned on me all of a sudden with his derringer."

"You didn't have no choice," a man said.

"Good riddance, I say," another man concurred.

"You done the right thing," a third man said. "Only thing you could do, somebody whips out a derringer on you like that."

Crowds had always scared Tully.

All crowds were potential lynch mobs, Tully believed, whether they were crowds of children, crowds of nuns, or crowds of boozers.

But this crowd seemed surprisingly docile.

As yet, Tully didn't have any idea what had happened here, but there was a curious calm about the people, including even the inebriated ones.

None of the saloons paid any deference to what was happening in the street. The player pianos continued to plink away, roulette wheels continued to whirl, and pathetic, toothless, old codgers continued to pledge their love to saloon gals who hadn't been checked recently for VD.

Mack Byrnes was standing over a dead man.

The dead man was Langley.

"Hi, Mack."

Byrnes had been staring down at Langley. He looked miserable: nervous, maybe even a little scared.

"I wish this was you standing here instead of me, Ben," Mack said quietly.

"What the hell happened?"

Byrnes told him.

"Why were you taking him to the jail?"

"Lawson told you he saw somebody at your place that night. I thought maybe he'd recognize Langley."

Tully was surprised. "So you're going to keeping looking into it?"

"Yeah, I guess I am."

"The mayor and the boys aren't going to like that."

Byrnes just shrugged. "They hired me to be a lawman. That's what I'm going to be.

"I appreciate it, Mack."

"I liked her, too, Ben. Remember that. And so did Susan."

"What the hell ever happened between them anyway? I never did understand that. They just had some kind of argument. Kate wouldn't talk about it, and neither would Susan."

"You got me. They wouldn't talk to me about it, either." Byrnes stared at the dead man.

"I don't feel good about this, Ben."

"He didn't leave you any choice."

"I don't want to get a reputation."

"You won't."

"Lawmen with a reputation . . . they're the ones all the killers come after."

The wagon from the funeral parlor clattered up. Somebody had gotten word to them right quick.

A buxom, sixteen-year-old girl with her hair up in braids and wearing a dusty white shirt and an even dustier pair of britches jumped down and said, "Need one of you men to help me pitch him in the buckboard here."

Tully smiled. "I see June Marie still isn't much for standing on ceremony."

Byrnes looked relieved for the light remark. "She's even more cold-blooded than her pa. And he's been plantin' people for forty years."

"C'mon," June Marie said, "one of you lazybones come over here and help me."

She had an intimidating way about her, and one man responded accordingly.

"Just grab him by the ankles," June Marie said, "and then I'll get him by the shoulders, and we'll throw him into the wagon."

And she meant *throw*.

June Marie and one of the men literally flung Langley up onto the wagon. The whole contraption shimmied when he hit.

There was at least a possibility Langley now had a couple of broken bones.

June Marie dusted her hands off and climbed back up on the board seat and moved the clattering wagon away.

"I sure hope she doesn't get her hands on me when my time comes," Tully said.

The crowd was drifting back to the saloon.

Byrnes said, "I guess I'd better be gettin' over to the office, Ben." He shook his head again. "My first night on the job as marshal, and I kill a man."

He sounded whipped.

# FOUR

TULLY DECIDED TO stick to tea that night. There were times when alcohol was good for his soul and times when it was bad. When it was good—at least every once in a while—he understood things he never had before. Small insights, admittedly, but the alcohol tended to clarify thoughts he'd been confused about. And sometimes liquor helped him appreciate beauty in everyday things. He'd gotten pissed while fishing one time, just sitting on a grassy bank a couple of feet above the river, and there in the sunlight he'd seen a frog. Never before had he ever truly *see* a frog. Not this way, anyway. What a magnificent—this was not to say attractive—creature it was, so complex and yet downright elegant in its mechanical simplicity. Frogs. Masterpieces of God's design.

But then liquor could turn him sour and ugly at times, too, especially lately when he looked back on his life with Kate and realized how much she'd deceived him.

Drink could make him think thoughts of her he never wanted to have. He'd loved her so truly, so purely that he'd hoped for a time—this after Langley had told him about her—that he'd find some explanation someday for why she'd kept her past to herself.

Because she'd now undermined every feeling he had for her.

Had she just tolerated him? Maybe she'd even found him disgusting. Tully could see how a woman like that would find him disgusting. He was and always would be just a prairie boy who'd picked up a ragbag of town words and attitudes to get by in civilization. But he'd always be something of a bumpkin, no doubt about that.

Had she and Langley laughed about him? Had she had to think about somebody else when they were making love? Had all his doting on her made him pathetic and foolish in her eyes?

He remembered times early on in their courtship when they'd be walking down the street and people would seem surprised to see them together. She was so pretty and, in her way, refined and he . . . Well. they were just surprised was all, woman like her choosing a man like him, even if he was a lawman and earned a fair if not spectacular wage.

He'd always suspected that he was a foolish man and when he got in these moods, drink only confirmed his suspicions.

Nor would drink clarify his feelings about Nan Conners.

Wasn't he being foolish about her, too?

He'd barely known her. Might not even have liked her—or she him—in different circumstances. And yet he'd felt this desperate sense of *belonging* with her. They stood against the world together.

But wasn't that the same sense he'd once had of Kate and himself?

The two of them—just the two of them—always together . . .

Thinking all these things as he sat there now, he went against his better judgment, stood up, walked to the table where he kept his whiskey, opened a new pint, carried it back to his rocking chair, and proceeded to get shit-faced to the lonely music of coyotes and wolves and night birds.

He was definitely a foolish, foolish man.

• • •

Tully had forgotten the pleasures of drunken sleep. Getting up to piss. Constantly waking up. Reconstructing the final hour of blurry wakefulness . . .

And hangover. Lovely hangover.

He wasn't that old a fella, but he was apparently old enough to feel the liquor a lot more than he used to. Dehydration. Headache. Disorientation. A twitching in the hands and fingers. A sick feeling not only in his stomach but in his whole body, a feverish, infirm sort of feeling.

He did the only thing he could think of. He ran stark naked to the river behind his cottage and dove in.

Now, there was a quick way to start dealing with your hangover. Freezing your ass (not to mention your balls) off and shimmying, shuddering, quaking to full awareness.

He swam around, none too skillfully, for somewhere in the vicinity of fifteen minutes. The way he was shivering, he felt he would never be warm again. Never.

He ran straight for the cottage, hugging himself as he did so.

An hour, three cups of coffee, and two cigarettes later, he saddled his horse and rode into town.

He had come to a decision somewhere during the bleak, boozy hours of last night, a decision that was professional rather than personal.

He didn't feel exactly good about it, but then he didn't feel exactly *bad* about it, either. It was going to surprise the folks of Pine City just as much as it had surprised him.

The telegraph office was busy. Always was in midmorning.

Tully went over to the table where you stood to compose your telegrams. He used a pencil. He knew what he wanted to write and wrote it swiftly. He didn't want time to maybe change his mind.

That was telegram number one, addressed to Mr. H. K. Neely, Attorney General's office.

Then he composed an even briefer second telegram.

Dear Sis,

Thought I'd come see you, Clem, and the boys for a while.

Train will get me there in three days. Will stay in a hotel.

Don't make any fuss.

Ben

He went to the café and had a formidable breakfast. Sending the telegrams had made him hungry. He felt unburdened. Alive to the soft almost-spring day and the needs of his belly.

His next stop was William L. D. Kimball, a round, dark-suited man who never got tired of his endless inappropriate smile, even if you did.

He told Kimball what he wanted to do, and Kimball said, "Well, now, Marshal, I do have to say this comes as a surprise."

Tully was glancing at the window just then. The word was Realtor, though from Tully's chair it read Rotlaer. Backwards.

"First of all, I'm not marshal anymore, And second of all, I don't have much use for it now that I'm alone."

"It should bring a pretty penny. Your Kate took good care of that place."

*Your Kate,* he thought. There had been a time when that phrase would've comforted him greatly. *My Kate. Yes indeed.*

"Here's my sister's address. You can get hold of me there."

"Didn't know you had a sister, Marshal."

There was no use correcting this officious little man. Tully would always be Marshal to most folks hereabouts.

"Yeah," Tully said, "and a nice one, too."

From there he started dropping into various places and saying his good-byes. Everybody seemed surprised to hear what he was doing until they heard him out, and then they had to agree that what he was doing made a lot of sense.

He sat in the back pew of the church for a time, watching

the sunbeams become brilliant colors as they angled through
the stained glass windows, listening to the whispers of the
old ladies at the little alcove where they prayed the statue of
the Virgin Mary; noting the progress of an arthritic old man
as he made his painful way around the stations of the cross.

After the church came the graveyard up on the windy hill
where Kate was buried. He knelt in front of her gravestone
and made the sign of the cross. He wasn't sure he remembered correctly the two prayers she always said but he gave
them a try and came pretty darned close.

He wanted to speak to her as one speaks to the dead, but
he couldn't speak to her with a pure heart—there were now
too many doubts about their whole time together—so he just
wished her well and said that wherever she was, she was
most likely in the hands of the Lord, which he meant.

Now it was time for home again. And packing. He had to
sort through all the things they'd accumulated over their
married years. He planned to size everything down to two
carpetbags.

Mack Byrnes sat in front of the door, smoking a cigarette
and playing with Sundown.

When Mack saw Tully coming, he stood up, brushed off
the seat of his jeans, and waved. He dropped his cigarette to
the grass and toed it out.

Tully dismounted.

"Figured you'd be along," Mack said.

"Been waiting long?"

Mack shrugged. "Not long. Came right out after I heard
about the telegrams you sent."

"The mayor and his boys send you, did they?"

"Nope. Took it upon myself to do it."

As Tully led the way inside, he laughed. "Figured that
telegram would be public information about five minutes
after it was sent."

"You don't have to leave town, you know."

"I know. Whiskey?"

"No, thanks."

Tully said. "Yeah, I guess I don't need any, either," He looked around. "Train's in four hours. I've got to start packing."

"I'll just watch."

Tully set about his work. He made two piles. Things he planned to keep, things he didn't. "Will you take care of Sundown for me? Anything else I leave behind, I want you and Susan to have."

"Appreciate it." Then: "Any way I can talk you out of this crazy bullshit?"

Tully kept making piles of things. "What crazy bullshit would that be?"

"Leaving town."

"It's time."

"So you don't give a damn who murdered Kate anymore?"

"That's why I sent the telegram to the investigator," Tully said. "I'm all caught up in this. Way too close to everything and everybody. Maybe he can figure it out. I can't. And I'm tired of trying."

"So you're just walking away?"

Tully paused, looked at him. "So I'm just walking away, Mack." He tossed a couple of shirts on the keep pile. "It bother you that the investigator might be coming back?"

"Doesn't bother me. But it's going to bother the mayor and Donnelly and Sieversen."

"You'll work with him? With the investigator?"

"Sure."

"You're going to get a lot of heat from the mayor."

"I know. But since I didn't have anything to do with lynching the wrong man, I don't have a dog in this race. If my hunch is right, by the way, I think we'll find out that Langley was actually the killer."

"I'm leaning in that direction myself."

Mack came over and angled himself right in front of Tully. "Are you sure there's no way I can change your mind? Susan said we'd be happy to have you stay with us for a while."

"I appreciate the offer, But it's time for me to move on."

"I figured that's what you'd say."

Tully nodded to the mess and mass of items strewn across the bed. "I've really got to get down to it, Mack."

Mack nodded. "So long, Ben."

The men shook hands.

Tully got down to serious, uninterrupted work.

# FIVE

TULLY TOOK HIS last look at Pine City as he rode into town, carpetbags slung across his saddle horn. Funny how towns could sneak up on you. You could live in a place a long time and never quite think of it as home. Think of it as just one more stopping-off place in your life. But then for one reason or another you had to leave it, and all of a sudden you realized that you'd actually miss the old place and a lot of the people, good people, and that it had been a real home after all,

He made his way to the livery. They'd give him a few dollars for his horse and see to it that the animal was bought by somebody who'd care well for it. People came up to him with outstretched hands, wanting to shake and say goodbye. He liked it. He just wished he was better at being social, at accepting compliments with grace rather than awkwardness and embarrassment.

The interior of the livery was shadowy in the mild, sunny morning, smelling sweetly of horseshit, hay, and the burning tobacco in a couple of old men's corncob pipes.

He saw the hand who was running the place—the owner off having breakfast "down to the café"—and made a deal on his horse. He patted the animal a couple of times and clung a moment or two longer than he maybe should have to the neck of the animal. ("You shoulda seen the marshal, all broke up over sayin' good-bye to his horse," he could hear the hand saying to folks.) He didn't like theatrics, and he didn't like grand exits. But when the hand was called by a customer to the front of the livery, Tully did give the animal a sort-of kind-of kiss on the neck. He'd been a damned good and reliable friend.

In the sunlight again, walking toward the depot, hands filled with the carrying straps of the carpetbags, he said a few more good-byes, accepted a kiss from a baby held up to him by a beaming mother, and even heard a few kind words from three of the town's sad, perpetual drunks who had just woken up in an alley.

He was maybe a quarter block from the depot when he heard someone call his name. He figured it was just one more well-wisher.

But when he turned, he was surprised to see that it was the nurse who'd been caring for O'Shea. She wore her white uniform, looking formal and imposing in the sunny day.

"I tried to find you all morning," she said breathlessly. She'd been running to catch him. "Didn't know if it was important or not, but Doctor O'Shea finally remembered whose horse it was he took care of that night."

"You going to get in trouble for telling me?"

"You mean Dobbins, my supervisor? She won't be any trouble." The nurse touched his arm, smiled. "As long as you never tell anybody I told you."

"That's a safe bet. My train leaves in just a little while. And I'll be taking all my secrets with me."

So she told him.

Right there in the dusty street. Right in the middle of all the morning commotion. The racket and rattle of wagons and buckboards and buggies, the shouts and laughter and chatter of workaday folks, a dozen little human moments—some sad, some funny, most just routine—being played out in the usual ways in this most usual of all mornings.

Except when the nurse said it, all the clatter, all the human noise seemed to fade. And the people seemed to pale to invisibility. He seemed to be standing alone on a vast pinnacle buffeted not by wind but by a single name echoing and echoing in his ears.

A few minutes later, the livery hand looked up and said, "Heck, Marshal, I figured you'd be on your train by now."

Tully said, "Yeah, I thought I would be, too." He dropped his carpetbags in a pile on the floor and said, "Keep an eye on these for me, all right?" He nodded to the back. "I'm going to need my horse again, too. I'll get him saddled up myself."

And then it was there. Unbidden. But vivid, undeniable.

The memory of that night. Following the Tully woman. As he had been secretly following her for days, weeks.

And sneaking into her house when she went out to the creek for some water. And waiting for her when she came back. And grabbing her then.

And then the knife—almost forgetting he had the knife—and then it was magically in his hand. And magically—oh my God, this couldn't really have been *him* doing it, could it?—jabbing it again and again into her chest, her throat, her belly, the pattern of the stabbings making no sense at all, just ramming the knife in wherever he could.

Unlike his other killings, there was no satisfaction in this one. There had been sexual fulfillment in the other women he'd killed, but this one—

But then how did the young girl get there?

*(He is dreaming this and, as with most dreams, images appear and disappear and reappear, images that beg any sort of sense or comprehension.)*

He was certain for that moment that he killed her.

Oh, yes, he killed her. Stabbing her over and over again.

And the strange emptiness afterward.

Was the emptiness because he didn't actually *stab* her but

only *thought* he had? Or wished he had? How else could he explain that he took no pleasure in this particular killing?

*The girl . . . .*

*The girl is the one with the knife.*

*It is she who stabs the Tully woman over and over.*

He first sees her when he sneaks into the Tully house, following in the footsteps of the Tully woman herself.

*The girl was apparently waiting for the Tully woman inside, in the darkness. And when the other girl appearing at the doorway.*

*Both girls are screaming vile things at the Tully woman as the one stabs her.*

*Accusing the Tully woman of destroying their family.*

*Accusing the Tully woman of sleeping with the girls' father.*

*"You're killing my mother!" one girl screams. "Don't you realize that!"*

*And then they're both stabbing her and stabbing and stabbing her. . . .*

And all he can do is watch, the knife-wielding girls just ignoring him standing in the doorway there.

But which version is the true one?

Did he kill the Tully woman, or did the girls?

Things are so confusing sometimes. You think you did something, but then it proves to be only a dream. And then sometimes you *do* do something . . . you're not sure you did.

It's as if somebody else did . . .

Or some part of you that you can't control, some part of you that waits for liquor to unlock it, some part of you that follows women and kills them.

The scream is real.

And downstairs, when Ralph Donnelly hears it, he realizes that he's never heard such a scream from his brother.

And then he is rushing up the stairs.

And smashing through his brother's closed door.

And seeing . . . something . . . his mind, at least in this initial moment, cannot reckon with: his brother's hand nailed to the wall with a nail the size of a railroad spike and him trying to pull his hand free.

Susan was tending to the lambs when Tully came over the grassy rise leading to the Byrnes homestead. On his way out here, he'd stopped by the marshal's office to talk to Mack, but they'd told him Mack was running some errands before he headed home. His afternoon off.

Susan seemed to know instantly why he was here. He was supposed to be on a train by now, leaving his old life and memories behind him. And besides, there was something about the way Tully sat in his saddle as he approached. Not the usual big circus wave and grin, sitting straight and stiff with no wave, big or small, at all.

She scattered the lambs and just stood there watching him dismount and walk over to her. She looked worn of her youth and beauty, and yet she was still attractive in her faded way. Prairie sweet and prairie hard.

"Afternoon, Ben."

"Hello, Susan." He hesitated. "You know why I'm here."

"Now, why would you say that?"

"We're friends, Susan, remember? We've known each other a long time. You should see your face. You're scared, and you're sad because I figured it out. Figured out some of it, anyway."

She brushed a lank piece of graying hair from her forehead. "I was hoping you'd get on the train and never find out."

"Why'd he kill her?"

"I'm gonna let you talk to Mack about that, Ben. That's not my place."

"Mack isn't here."

"He is now."

She nodded to the rise Tully had just come up.

Mack was just at the peak of that rise now, coming home. He'd be thinking of a warm meal and some pleasant time with his wife and girls. Maybe a little hunting this afternoon after a nice, leisurely, afternoon-off nap.

They both watched him approach. Neither said a word.

He ground-tied his horse same way Tully had and then came forward with a wide grin. "Hell, man, don't tell me you're going to stay. That's great."

Mack Byrnes was a lot of good things, but an actor he wasn't.

All weary Susan said was, "He knows, Mack."

There was a wind still with winter on it and it was as bleak as Susan's gaze.

"You killed my wife, Mack."

And all Mack said was, "Yeah, I did."

"You hid in the timber behind my house. Your horse got scraped up. The vet told me."

Susan broke. No warning. Just broke. Sobbing so loud the wind must've taken the sound across the sea, all the way to England. Just broke, her little body so aggrieved it looked as if it would collapse in on itself.

Mack went to her. Took her in his arms. So she'd known, too. And now Tully wondered about something else. Susan and Kate such good friends for so long, and then suddenly not on speaking terms. Had there been something between Kate and Mack that Susan had found out?

"At least it's over with, honey. You were sick of waiting for Ben to find out, and so was I. At least it's over with. I'll get a good lawyer. Things'll be all right."

By this time, the girls, who had been inside the house, had heard their mother's weeping and came running toward her.

They wrapped their arms around her and hugged her; they were almost as one piece, all of them, clinging together there in the prairie wind this way, a hawk arcing down the sky just now. He could almost pity Mack at this moment. Almost.

Mack pulled away first. Louise grabbed her father's sleeve and began sobbing as loudly as her mother.

Tully felt sick, enraged, betrayed, sorrowful. Tully felt like shit.

"You stay with your mother, honey," Mack said softly to

Louise. He hugged her, kissed her on the forehead, and gently pushed her into the waiting arms of her sister, Delia.

Delia raised her elegant head and began to say something to Tully, but her father snapped, "You take care of your sister and your mother. There's been enough talk."

He turned to Tully. Took his Colt from his holster and handed it over. Then he took a pair of handcuffs from his belt and handed those to Tully, too. He pushed his hands together and waited for Tully to cuff him.

"I can't take them crying, Tully," he whispered. "I've ruined their lives. No matter how much you hate me, please get me out of here. This is worse than the gallows."

Tully thought of going over to Susan and the girls and trying to say something soothing. But hell, it would be just as empty as an undertaker's words when you were peering into the box.

Less than two minutes later, the two men rode out. Neither one looked back.

So Mack told him about it, or a lot of it anyway, on the ride back to town.

Tully didn't get mad. He got—what?—something he'd never felt before. Some kind of dead-inside feeling. He listened with the dispassion of a stranger hearing a saloon tale.

Mack'd stopped out a few times to see Tully, who turned out not to be home—"I didn't have anything in mind, Ben, I really didn't"—and from time to time, Kate'd just drop little hints that she was sort of unhappy. Then she eventually told him about Langley and what a bastard he was but how she couldn't get him out of her mind.

By this time, Mack had become her confidante—"I guess I knew I was falling in love with her, and I knew I should pull away, but I didn't, Ben, and God knows I should've; God knows, considering what I've done to you and my family"—and she told him that she really respected Tully a lot and was grateful to him but that she didn't love him. She needed some "spice" in her life. She could see her looks starting to fade, and she was starting to feel old.

And that's how Mack was feeling. Trapped. His life over. Some "spice" would be nice.

And so they gave each other spice.

Mack didn't delude himself. He loved her, but she didn't love him. (He spared Tully the fact that their sex was good, but Tully was smart enough to sense that for himself.)

This went on for six, seven months, and then one day Susan found a picture he'd been stupid enough to filch from the marshal's desk.

Susan confronted Kate; that was why they never spoke afterward. They both agreed not to tell Tully. They'd go on with their lives.

But home life was miserable. Susan knew Mack no longer loved her. And the girls heard them fight every night and went to bed crying.

And then Mack started slipping back, seeing Kate again. And that's when Langley showed up and caught them. Langley said he'd tell Tully unless he got one hell of a lot of money from Mack, which was why Mack held up the stage for the Carter jewels and cash. And when Mack killed Langley taking him in, Langley really had tried to pull his derringer on him, but Mack was too fast for that. Mack really had been defending himself.

Mack took a deep sigh. "Night I killed Kate, I went there as usual, and everything seemed fine. And then she said she wanted to break it off, that she was probably going to meet up with Langley in St. Louis first chance she got. And then I killed her. I saw the knife on the table there, and I just started stabbing her with it."

They rode on in silence.

Just when they reached town, Mack said, "You going to say anything, Ben?"

"Nothin' to say," Tully said, looking straight ahead. "Nothin' to say at all."

Tully took up his old office. Nobody complained. He put Mack Byrnes in a cell and then sent for Steve Kepler, the night man. Kepler was there in fifteen minutes, sleepy-eyed but gunning steaming black coffee to wake up. He usually slept 'til early afternoon. His wife was about to have a kid. His days of sleeping in would soon end.

Tully said Kepler would now have to become acting marshal and told him why.

"You think I can handle it?"

"You'll have to, Steve."

"How about you, Ben? You could come back."

"There's another train out in about four hours. I'll be on it."

"I'm sorry for you, and I'm sorry for Mack." He looked young and confused.

"I probably shouldn't say that about Mack."

"It's all right. I guess I feel sorry for him, too. As much as I'd like to kill the sonofabitch. You should've seen Susan and the girls."

"I'm glad I didn't. Think of what their lives're gonna be now."

Tully nodded.

"So Mack must've killed Nan Conners, too."

"She was forcing his hand. That's what he told me. Forcing the issue again. And eventually people would figure out that he'd killed my wife."

"I'm still sorry about your wife, Ben. I liked her."

"Yeah, I did, too," Tully said. And smiled sadly. "And I still do, even after everything I've heard."

"It's funny sometimes, ain't it? How you still like people who hurt you? Don't make any sense."

Commotion out front. A familiar, booming voice.

His Honor the mayor.

They were telling him that he couldn't just walk back to the marshal's office, even though he was the mayor; they were telling him to have a seat in the front, and they'd go get Tully; they were telling him that he should calm down and have a cup of coffee.

But all he told them was to go to hell and to fuck off and to be careful, or he'd see to it that they got their asses fired from their lazybones jobs of theirs.

And then he was in the doorway, His Honor, all fury and furor, and saying, "This is preposterous, and you know it, Tully! Mack Byrnes didn't kill your wife any more than I did."

Tully took great pleasure in seeing the man's consternation. His world was collapsing. They'd lynched an innocent man, and now they would have to face their mistake.

"Care for some coffee, Mayor?"

The mayor came in and slammed the door behind him.

"Why the hell'd you bring him in, anyway?"

"Because he confessed."

"Confessed?" The man seemed sincerely surprised. "He confessed?"

"Yes, he did. And he confessed to killing Nan Conners, and he confessed to sticking up the stage with the Carter jewels and money on it."

The bluster was replaced by a baffled tone. The mayor sat down slowly in a chair and said, "He couldn't have killed your wife, Tully."

"Why not?"

"Because the afternoon of the day she died, the old stage bridge collapsed, and Mack had to go out there and fix it with a couple other people. You know how handy he is."

"That doesn't mean he didn't kill her."

The mayor looked at Tully as if Tully were a dolt. "Tully, Mack and the other three men left town here just after noon. They were together until about four the next morning, working on the bridge. Together, Tully. You know what that means? There's no way Mack could've killed her. And I've got three honest, upstanding men who'll testify to that."

A few seconds later, the same kind of commotion that had ushered in the mayor now ushered in Ralph Donnelly. "I'm capable of walking back there myself!"

Just hearing the voice and looking over at the mayor reminded Tully of why he'd wanted to leave this town. For all the people he liked, for all the ways he'd come to see it as home, there was still the problem with the people who owned and ran the town, a yoke no decent lawman should have to labor under.

Donnelly burst into Tully's office and said, "You're determined to take this whole town down with you, aren't you, Tully?"

"All I want's the truth, Ralph."

"The truth? Now doesn't that sound high and mighty. The truth. The virtuous marshal versus the bad townspeople." He slipped into the chair next to His Honor.

"Not the bad townspeople, Ralph. Just the crooks who run it."

"I resent that!" the mayor said.

"I don't give a shit if you resent it or not, gentlemen. You hanged an innocent man. And you've done everything you can to cover that up."

"Well, maybe we did hang an innocent man, Tully. But you just *jailed* an innocent man."

"That's what I was telling him, Ralph. There's no way Mack Byrnes could've killed Tully's wife. He was with some other boys out to the stage bridge that night."

Donnelly slid a silver flask of whiskey from his back pocket—Tully had never seen him drink during the day before—hoisted it, and took a heavy dose.

"I'm gonna share something with you two, but I'm not gonna tell you where I got it from. And I don't want no questions about it, all right? But it's the truth. That's one thing I'm sure of."

"If it's the truth, why won't you tell us who you got it from?" the mayor said.

"Dammit, you want to hear this or not?"

"Let him talk," Tully said. "I want to hear this."

And when Donnelly said it, it sounded right. Unlikely, improbable, completely unexpected but right somehow.

Tully thought of what Mack had told him about how his affair with Kate had affected the family. All the fights. The bitterness. The grief. The family coming apart.

Yes, it sounded right.

Terribly, terribly right.

•   •   •

A few minutes later, as Tully left his office and headed to the cells in back, one of the deputies stopped him and said, "You was busy with the mayor and all, Marshal, so I just took 'em back myself."

Tully pretty much guessed who he was going to see when he got back there. And his guess proved right.

"Hello, girls," he said.

The other cells were empty. Mack stood with his big hands gripping the bars of his cage. He'd been crying, and so had the girls.

"Get them out of here, Ben," he said. "Please."

"Where's your mom, girls?" Tully said.

"She don't know we're here," Louise said.

"We kind've snuck off," Delia said.

"Did you hear what I asked you, Ben? Will you please get these girls out of here? I don't want them to see me here."

Tully stayed calm. He said, "Were you girls planning to come and see me?"

Delia nodded.

Louise said, "We wanted to see pa first. Talk to him a little."

"Ben, please—" Mack said.

"You two killed Kate, didn't you?" Tully said. "And Nan Conners?"

"We're sorry we did, Marshal," Delia said softly. "It was just seeing our home life all torn apart . . ."

She took a step closer and touched his arm. "I'm sorry, Marshal. I really am."

Mack said, "This is all my fault, Ben. All my fault."

And then he was on his bunk, weeping into his hands.

Tully didn't know what to say, do, think.

He was not a wise man. He survived day to day. He tried to be as decent in his life as circumstances allowed, but something like this was far beyond his ability to deal with in any way.

Two married people start sleeping together . . . and so many lives are destroyed.

"This is all my fault," Mack said miserably, over and over again.

Tully led the girls out of the jail and back up to his office, where the mayor and Donnelly sat talking quietly.

After he ushered the girls inside, he said, "You folks all need to talk. I've got a train to catch."

# SIX

HE MIGHT HAVE been a youngster, the way his body leaned toward the oncoming train. Head full of hope, eyes full of wonder, standing there all raw and vulnerable after everything that had happened here in Pine City. Alone on the depot platform, eager to be gone.

He carried his two carpetbags on board and then found himself a seat. Thank God for the invention of the Pullman car. For the first time, rail travel was a true pleasure.

And now the train pulled away, all that fierce power, and he settled back in his seat and closed his eyes, startled to find that he could slip so readily into sleep. . . .

And they were all waiting for him in his sleep, in his dreams: Kate and Nan, Mack and Susan, Delia and Louise, and the whole town of them, the mayor and Donnelly and Sieversen. . . .

The wonderful smell of perfume woke him. His first guess was that the scent was somehow part of his dreams.

But when he looked over at the young, elegant woman sitting next to him—a prim and yet somehow erotic face—he realized that she was quite real.

"I'm sorry I woke you. This was the only empty seat."